Witchy Woman

The Pruitt Witches Book Two

Zoe Shae

This book is a work of fiction. While some places or people are real—Chagrin Falls, Ohio being an example—most names, characters, places, and incidents either are products of the author's imagination or used fictitiously.

WITCHY WOMAN

ZOE SHAE

Cover design: Luisa Sipia, @luy_co

Editing: Jax at Starry-Eyed Scribbles, and Dewi Hargreaves

For information of subsidiary rights, please contact the author at authorzoeshae@gmail.com

ALSO BY ZOE SHAE

Standalones:

Sugar

The Pruitt Witches Series:

Spell Ya Later

Witchy Woman

Third book Coming Soon!

To those labeled difficult, unlikeable, or hard to love. There's more to your story, and I see you.

Thank you for picking up Witchy Woman. If you don't want any spoilers and are okay with the possibility of being triggered, please skip this page. If, however, you would like to avoid certain triggering topics, here is a list of the ones that appear in this book. Please protect your own mental health.

- Death
- Depictions of Hell
- Explicit/offensive language
- Cancer references
- Referenced past murder
- Referenced violence
- Burn marks/injuries

CHAPTER 1

ONCE UPON A TIME

There's one thing in my life that I am absolutely clear on.

I do not want a soulmate.

It doesn't matter that my family is 'blessed' by some long-dead witchy ancestor, so I have one by default. It doesn't matter that I've already met him.

I have free will, and I don't want a soulmate.

I'm quite happy not dealing with any of the excessive drama that seems to follow the entire concept of soulmates around like a cloud.

It's only been a month since Noah got kidnapped and it practically destroyed Hazel. And that's without even mentioning the death of my father, who was literally killed by a warlock because he was my mother's soulmate.

Soulmates are more trouble than they're worth.

Grandma never met her soulmate and she's just fine. And I'll live without mine and be just fine.

Despite the fact I think about him constantly.

Especially when I'm here at the witches' market where I first met him, when I delivered a package from my grandmother to his booth. My boots crunch on the semi-frozen ground. Winter is fast approaching in Chagrin Falls, Ohio, and I'm expecting our first snowfall any day now. Regardless of the cold—and any daydreams about a soulmate I don't want—I'm not wasting the opportunity to come to the magic market.

On any given day there's between twenty-five and one hundred booths selling anything I could imagine. Fashion, accessories, spellbooks, food, herbs, talismans, art. The possibilities are endless. The smells should clash with each other, but somehow they form a cohesive scent that has a warm, wintery, spicy undertone. It's comforting.

The market is a little threadbare as we go into winter. Makes sense, really, but it's a shame to see it less busy. It's easier to get lost when there's a crowd to get lost in.

"There's my Goldilocks," a rough, gravelly voice says in my ear.

And there's the reason I would like to be lost in a crowd.

Ash Cedar.

The scent of warm fires, evergreen trees, and musk hits me as he leans in so close I can feel his breath tickle my ear. My soulmate.

Not that he knows that. Or ever will, if I have any fucking say in it.

"Can I help you?" I ask, resisting turning to face him.

"I haven't been told I'm an overgrown brute today," he chuckles. The warmth of his body is overwhelming, making me want to lean in and soak it up like a cat in the sun. "I missed it."

"Surprising considering how insufferable you are."

"There it is." He circles me, coming to a stop in front of me.

He's a gigantic bear of a man—lumberjack-core to the extreme—so it almost hurts my neck to look up at him. But I want to make eye contact. I won't give him the satisfaction of seeing me flinch. Even if it's difficult not to notice how his black Henley strains against the muscles of his arms and chest.

I cross my arms, matching his emerald-green stare with one of my own. "Is there anything else I can help you with or did you just need to satisfy your degradation kink?"

His face lights up, a broad smile erupting underneath his short beard. "Say 'kink' again, Goldilocks."

"You're disgusting. And predictable. Boring, even." I quirk an eyebrow. "I could forgive the rudeness, but being boring? I can't forgive that."

There's fire in his eyes. "The last thing I am is boring."

The dark timbre of his voice, the promise behind his words, chases my annoyance away, replacing it with pure heat. He would make me melt in his arms in moments, of that I have no doubt.

But I don't melt. And I don't do soulmates.

"As fun as this has been, I have things to do that don't include verbally sparring with a lumberjack. Lovely as always, Mr. Cedar."

I turn tail and flee as fast as I can without running.

I don't imagine the dark chuckle chasing behind me.

I weave my way through the people, through families bundled up in their matching jackets, and feel a pang in my chest. Happy families always do that to me, though.

My gait slows as I come upon Hazel's booth. It's not completely set up yet, but she comes here multiple times a week to get it ready for the new year. She's an artist and is going to sell her magical moving paintings.

A ripple of jealousy comes unbidden. My sister, the used-to-be hermit, is out here casually using magic to make all her dreams come true.

She's found herself and her magic. It's great. She just abandoned me to do it, then let me know in no uncertain terms that I was the reason she had nothing in her life.

The lion, the witch, and the audacity of this bitch.

I walk up to one of the paintings on display. It's of Lake Erie, a view that you can find close to the coast outside of Cleveland. A spot I showed her. A spot I dragged her to because she used to barely ever leave the house.

And here she is selling a painting of it, her magic causing the waves to lap at the shore.

How did this happen? I was the confident sister. I was the one who knew exactly what she wanted out of life. I was the one who got out of the house and dated boys and was fucking headed toward something.

I was going to finish community college and go to fashion school—design hats, scarves, maybe some jewelry, too. I was going to escape this stupid small town and my fucked-up family, maybe move to London or Paris.

But that dream died a fiery death the minute Hazel stomped out of the house and changed our lives forever.

Now, the roles are completely reversed. Hazel has her soulmate Noah, she has her passion, she's starting a business, and she has a backbone. Confidence.

She sacrificed me to get all of that. She threw me to the wolves without a single look back. Mom forced me to drop out of college, saying she couldn't protect Hazel anymore but that she wouldn't lose both of us. I couldn't see my friends anymore. She actually stole my fucking car keys at one point.

But does Hazel know any of this? No. She didn't care enough to ask.

"Hey, you!" Hazel pops up beside me. "Find anything?"

Asking me about shopping? She's obviously feeling guilty. She doesn't shrink into herself like she used to, but I can see that guilt written all over her face.

"Can we leave now?" I ask. I regret coming here with her, but I was hoping . . . I don't know what I was hoping. Maybe that coming here would distract me. Maybe that it would inspire me.

All it's done is remind me that I have a soulmate I need to stay away from, a life I hate, and a sister who I don't understand anymore.

Her face falls, concern knitting her auburn eyebrows together. "Okay."

HAZEL and I arrive back home in a flurry of bags. Her guilt has made her willing to help me carry everything upstairs.

Her guilt also means she's moved back in to the house from the apartment she was renting from Grandma. Which, in and of itself, isn't the worst thing in the world. But the house likes her.

I've always known the house is sentient, despite Hazel apparently just finding out, and I've enjoyed my conversations with it over the years.

When Hazel left, I would sit and talk to the house for hours. It was my way of pretending I wasn't completely isolated and it stopped me from calling my sister. It doesn't respond like a human would—I'm not a crazy person—but I've learned to decipher the creaks and moans. The way it would moan a little when I let the tears fall, or creak and crackle the floor when I made a joke.

But now that Hazel is back? The house pays attention to *both* of us, not just me. And I don't like it.

Speaking of inanimate talking objects, the candles in my bedroom flicker and pop as I drop my bags on my bed.

Fire whispers to me. I've never been able to understand the soft whisperings, and I've gotten good at ignoring it. When I first started hearing the mumbles as a preteen it scared the shit out of me, but I eventually figured it was fine because it never actually *said* anything. It couldn't be that bad if I wasn't actually hearing voices.

But not anymore. Not since Mom splashed away in a giant ball of water with her ex-boyfriend-slash-nemesis-slash-whatever-the-fuck-he-was Draven a month ago.

Whenever anyone brings up giving Mom a funeral, the fire says no. It says no so clearly that I can't mistake it for anything else.

I'm terrified of what else it might start saying.

"Laura!" Grandma calls from downstairs. "Dinner is ready!"

I don't bother replying, I just leave my things in bags and walk into the hallway and down the staircase.

Grandma has also been staying with us off and on since Mom. She likes to maintain her privacy so she will usually stay for three to four days, work on Mom's garden for a little bit, then leave for a week.

At the base of the staircase, I can see Grandma and Hazel's heads are buried together in the kitchen. They're conspiring so intently they don't even notice me despite being in plain view. Hazel always used to claim I was Grandma's favorite, and at one time that may have been true.

Not anymore.

Regardless, I'm hungry, and I'll endure whatever ridiculous plan they've put together for a taste of Grandma's pork roast.

I walk into the kitchen and grab a plate, startling the two of them. Jealousy rises like bile in my throat at their easy closeness. Closeness I used to have, closeness I don't have anymore.

Whatever. I don't care. Not when there's homemade perfection in the form of fall-apart pork roast, garlic mashed potatoes, roasted asparagus, and brown sugar-glazed carrots.

Fucking yum.

"How was the market today, girls?" Grandma asks once we're all seated. The antique table is worn on the edges from years of use, as are the matching wood chairs.

It feels weird that Mom isn't here. As much as I don't *want* her here, she had such a commanding presence. She took up so much space with her energy it's as if there's a black hole where her chair sits.

"Good!" Hazel pipes up. "I think I've got everything just about set for my booth next year."

Whoop-de-doo.

"Laura? What about you, dear?"

"It was fine, Grandma." It's so much fun being the boring sister.

I don't miss the look they share. The 'Oh, poor Laura, she's so damaged, what are we going to do about her?' look. It's infuriating. I scowl in their direction and stuff a forkful of mashed potatoes into my mouth.

"I have an idea I'd like to run past you," Grandma says. "I was wondering if you'd like to start magic lessons with me and Hazel. I think it'd be prudent for you to begin learning how to harness your magic."

"Oh, I'm finally invited to sit with the cool kids?" I snark. "Lucky me."

Anger grows in my chest like a molten bubble in a sea of lava, ready to pop.

"You were always invited to our lessons, Laura," Hazel says.

"I'm pretty sure my invitation got lost in the mail because I never received one."

"Laura," Grandma sighs. She's lost her fire since Mom. Once upon a time she'd be telling me to take my attitude and shove it. "It's imperative that you learn how to defend yourself. We have no idea how long it will take for Draven to form a plan and make his next move. Once he returns from being banished to Hell, he will come for each of us and I refuse to allow you both to be defenseless."

Defenseless. Her words remind me that I'm the only one of us who still doesn't know what the fuck they're doing. I'm the least prepared. The least connected to her magic.

I'm the failure.

The lava bubble pops.

"Well, if you two have already decided, then I don't have much say in the matter, do I?" I slap my hands on the table. "How about instead of presenting it as a choice, you tell me the truth. I'm going to magic lessons and that's that."

Grandma's eyebrow shoots up.

Good. Get annoyed. Get mad. Fight with me. Show me some sort of emotion instead of the passive bullshit I've been getting.

"You will go to magic lessons and that's that." Grandma

smiles, a snarky thing that makes me feel like I've fallen into a trap. "And you will work a booth for The Cat's Cradle at the market this winter."

The market? A lance of panic shoots through my false bravado. I can't be at the market every day. Not with him.

How long can I keep pushing him away if I'm literally forced to be around him every single day?

"Grandma, I—" I protest.

She holds her hand up to stop me. "That's final."

Hazel tries to open her mouth as well, but Grandma shoots her a glare. This topic is over.

How in the fuck did I end up in this mess?

"It seems I've lost my appetite." I stand, glaring at both of them before turning my back and stomping up to my room.

I'm not an idiot. I know exactly why they're so hell-bent on having me learn my magic. I'm not fond of the idea of Draven ripping me a new asshole either, but that doesn't mean I enjoy being ordered around like a dog.

Two knocks sound on my bedroom door.

Hazel pokes her head in. "Do you mind if I come in?"

"Not sure I have any free will anymore, so why not?" I snap.

Her smile is guilty as she walks in and sits across from me on the bright pink bedspread. "I'm sorry how that all went down downstairs. That definitely wasn't the plan."

"So you admit there was a plan? That you've been talking about me behind my back?" My hands fly up of their own accord. "Instead of involving me in decisions that affect myself and our family, you've been actively excluding me."

She has the decency to drop her eyes, at least. "Well, when you say it like that it does seem bad. It doesn't come from a bad place, though. I'm just worried about you. Worried about all of us, honestly."

"Worried about Noah?"

Noah. One of the main reasons I will not be engaging with my soulmate. Is Noah fantastic? Absolutely. The nerd is great. But did he also get kidnapped and nearly killed by the psycho warlock who killed my father? You're damn skippy.

And there's no way in fuck I am putting myself—or my soulmate—through that. I'll push him away until I can't push anymore to keep him safe from Draven. To keep myself from becoming another woman in this family who lost her soulmate. To keep myself from turning into Mom.

She nods. "Of course I am. He knows much more about what's going on now, but I think I'd lose it if anything happened to him again. I'd lose it if anything happened to you, too."

"I get it, okay? You have every right to be worried." I shuffle away from her. "But I'm an adult. Stop treating me like a child. I deserve to be part of those conversations."

"Okay." She exhales a deep breath that makes her seem so much older than her twenty-five years. Like she's truly been through some shit. And she has. "You're right. No more planning without you."

"Thank you."

She stands. "Oh, and Laura?"

I make a questioning noise as I pull out my sketchbook. It's full of designs for accessories I'll never make.

"Noah told me what you said on the phone with him after he and I had our falling out. How you convinced him to come and see me."

My body stills. I specifically told that man not to mention that we talked. One look from his soulmate and he sings like a fucking bird.

She approaches, coming a little too close to my personal bubble. "Thank you. I know we are in a weird place right now, but I love you. And I appreciate so much that you went to him."

Tears burn my eyes. Fuck her for making me cry. For reminding me that the person I felt safest with for most of my life is still right there but that things are so different between us now. There's a deep, scared little piece of my heart that just wants her big sister. But the part she hurt is bigger.

"Yeah," I sniffle. "Whatever. I was just sick of seeing you so miserable."

She chuckles and leaves the room, the door making a gentle *snick* behind her.

"I love you, too," I whisper to the empty space.

CHAPTER 2

GOLDILOCKS

The next morning I'm outside Grandma's shop, The Cat's Cradle, at eight thirty sharp. Hazel will be opening the shop while Grandma gets me situated at the market, but that doesn't mean we'll be having a late start.

The toe of my faux furry boot taps against the sidewalk as I shiver. That winter chill is cold as fuck, but there's no way I'm going inside. The first time I walked in there I was almost bowled over by disorienting memories I had long forgotten. Memories Mom stole from me, hid from me, with her magic. I can barely remember Dad outside of a few core memories, like him helping me blow out the candles at my birthday party and buying me my first sketchbook. I'd assumed I was too young to remember much else. But that wasn't it at all.

I have no interest in it happening again.

I still don't understand why Mom took my memories, but there's a lot of things about my life that I no longer understand.

And despite everything, I don't want to see the last place she walked free.

"Morning, dear!" Grandma steps out of her car. "I have most of the supplies already in the car but my favorite tablecloth is in the shop."

My arms cross my chest as another shiver wracks my body. "I'll wait here."

I don't miss the calculated eyes sweeping over me, or the raised eyebrow. "If you're sure."

Sure I don't want to go in the shop? Yes.

She opens the door to The Cat's Cradle as I turn to the town. My hometown. Chagrin Falls, Ohio. The shop sits on Main Street along with the other mostly brick buildings that line the road on either side. Boutiques, bookstores, and restaurants with people fluttering in and out. Their chatter tends to hide the sounds of the waterfalls themselves, but you can still hear them when it's quiet.

It's the most New England town outside of New England.

When we were younger, Dad used to take us to the Popcorn Shop overlooking the falls every Sunday afternoon to get us hopped up on sugar before family dinner. Thankfully, that memory wasn't stolen.

"I love this town in the winter," Grandma says, sneaking up behind me with the tablecloth underneath her arm. "I may not always love snow, but it adds a certain magical quality to everything."

"Yep. Let's go." The butterflies swirling in my belly are threatening to take over. I don't want to go to the market. I don't want to see Ash. I don't want any of this.

I just want my life back. Despite how broken it was, how fake it was, it was expected. Comfortable. Mine.

The car ride is quiet. Grandma doesn't know what to say to me anymore, and I don't know what to say to her. She's so fucked up by what happened to Mom I barely recognize her. It feels wrong to tease her when she's already so hurt, but teasing her was the way we talked to each other before.

Now it just feels cruel.

And I may be a bitch, but I'm not cruel.

We pull up to the field, which is completely empty to the naked eye, but actually covered by a magical veil that obscures the market from view. It's kept up by most of the witches who have stalls, including Grandma, and it also acts as a ward to keep out malevolent types and humans.

"Where are we setting up?" I ask.

Grandma waves her hands a little, securing her feet on the ground with a smile. Magic. The scent of it fills my nose. It's the heat of a bonfire on a summer evening, the scent of marshmallows and wood crackles. Pure warmth and comfort.

I watch as dirt slowly spreads at her feet; tendrils of tree roots twist together, forming one large tangle. The roots lift the boxes and bags in the car, waiting for Grandma's direction. "Come, come."

I follow Grandma and her personal tree-root butler through the magical barrier and into the bustle of the market. I won't be able to hide from Ash, not with my own booth. I'll be a sitting duck and he's going to torment me all he wants.

"Here we are!" Grandma says, fanning the deep, royal-purple tablecloth over the basic wooden table. Very bougie—very Grandma. It's thick and plush and ready to be decorated within an inch of perfection. "I like to arrange things in their categories. I have a few different display cases and decorative plates to make everything look nice. You can have creative control over that. I trust your taste."

Despite feeling like a grumpy monster, I preen at the compliment. Having good taste is something I take a lot of pride in, and knowing she agrees is validating. "I got this."

"I was thinking of doing a little shopping while you get set up. Is that all right with you? I can answer any questions when I return," Grandma says. "All the things you'll need are on the ground in well-labeled boxes."

Grandma is always well organized.

I nod in agreement, eager for a moment to myself. For a little space.

She leaves in a flourish of her dress, headed toward a flock of muumuu-wearing witches. I wrinkle my nose. Definitely not my style.

I pull one of the floral plates out, determined to organize crystals into a beautiful display, when I catch the gaze of a guy. A reasonably attractive guy, if I'm honest. Tall, blonde, fit.

But he's not Ash.

And apparently since I found my stupid soulmate, the thought of even kissing another guy makes me want to fucking barf.

Dating was one of my favorite activities. I loved the instant endorphin rush from meeting someone new, and the flame of chemistry was addicting. It may have burned bright and quick, but it was fun.

And I never wanted more than that. I never wanted to run the risk of suffering with the pain my mother did.

Stupid. Fucking. Soulmates.

I slam a crystal down a little too hard, the crackling *clink* against the plate jarring the relative silence of my small booth. I cringe. I'm trying to avoid bringing attention to myself, not plaster a neon sign over my head that says, 'Look at this stupid bitch.'

"Do you need help?" a masculine voice asks. I turn to find the guy—the perfectly attractive but totally barf-worthy guy—I made eye contact with. He's smiling at me with amusement and it's just . . . ick.

"No—" I start, but am interrupted by a deliciously large brute of a lumberjack wedging his way between me and the mystery man, his back to me so I can't see the expression on his face.

"She's fine. Move along," Ash Cedar says, voice booming with authority and no small amount of possessiveness.

My knees wobble as I have to physically restrain myself from melting into his back. Even that was hot, and isn't that frustrating?

The other man doesn't bother replying before he scampers away. Or at least, I assume he scampers based on the sound of shoes hustling away on cold, crunchy ground. I can't actually see anything around the massive Hulk-wannabe in front of me.

"Was that entirely necessary?" Despite my annoyance at my predicament flaring to life, I can't fully remove the breathless quality from my voice.

With a swagger I refuse to admit is sexy as hell, Ash slowly turns to me. His giant arms are crossed over his barrel chest as his green eyes sweep over me. "Yes."

"Maybe I wanted his help!"

I didn't. But Ash certainly doesn't need to know that.

"If you need help, Goldilocks, you ask *me*."

I huff out a frustrated breath. "Can you please do whatever Alpha A-hole crap this is somewhere else? I have a booth to set up."

A smile breaks across his face as if my resistance is purely amusing. "You're going to be working a booth here?"

Fuck.

"Grandma wants to have The Cat's Cradle set up at the market for the season," I reply.

"Goldilocks." He invades my space, the scent of warm fires, evergreen trees, and musk crawling underneath my skin. "That's not what I asked."

"I said I didn't need help."

His eyes flicker down to my lips, lingering there. "Nah, that's not what you said at all. You said you didn't need his help. You never said you didn't need mine. You want to put me to work? I'll do anything you tell me."

I raise a single eyebrow. "Anything?"

The smile melts from his face, a seriousness I haven't experienced from him overtaking his expression. "Tell me to lift boxes . . . arrange crystals. Tell me to get on my knees and crawl to you. I'll worship at your altar."

Heat blooms in my cheeks, spreading through my body and threatening to burn me alive. The mental image of this man on his knees is too much.

"And if I ask you to leave?" My voice trembles.

He nods. "Then I will. But not forever, Goldilocks. I'll always come back for you."

~

I SET up the rest of the booth in a fog. A lusty, anxiety-ridden fog. It would be one thing if my attraction to Ash was one-sided. Or if he was shy. But his obvious pursuit of me is beyond my ability to handle.

I want him to stop.

Don't I?

At the very least, I'm happy he respects me when I tell him to leave. He may not understand personal space, but he understands no.

That's more than I can say for a lot of people.

By the time I've finished, the booth is neat and orderly but my brain is a jumbled mess. Even though I can't see or hear Ash, I can still sense him. Sense the electric current that I only allowed myself to feel just once.

Right after Mom died.

We came to the market so Hazel could see the moving paintings and have her whole 'coming to Jesus' moment. For me, it was the first time Ash touched me. He didn't say a word, neither did I. I was with my family and all he did was brush my shoulder with his arm.

The electric shock was exactly as Hazel described it. Like sticking your finger in a socket. Sharp, brief, and full of everything I've never wanted.

Sure, maybe when I younger I wanted what my parents had. But there's no point in it. Not when losing it can turn you into the kind of person my mom is.

Was.

Is?

"The booth looks lovely, dear," Grandma says, snapping me out of my musings.

I smile. "Thank you."

"Since you're not as familiar with the shop, I made a little cheat sheet for you." She hands me a slip of paper. "The pricing is on that. Everything should be labeled well enough that you can put it all together. But I'll stay with you for your first week as you adjust. After that, if you need help you can always call me or Hazel."

"Do I get a paycheck for manning your booth like Hazel does for the store?" I ask. Partially because the urge to be snarky is too much to ignore, and partially because I haven't had a job in my life, and it would be nice to have some money. Mom would give me a little something to get lunch at the cafeteria on campus but nothing extra.

"Yes. You'll earn the same pay as Hazel does."

At least she and I are on equal footing in something.

"And remember, your first magic lesson is tonight. I expect you to be in the shop by no later than seven."

The shop? Uh, no. Nope. No thank you.

I shoot her my doe eyes. "Why can't we just do it at home? I'm sure the house would appreciate the magic."

"The house is just fine on its own." She stares me down. "We will meet in the shop. It has the correct space and energy."

How do I explain to her what that space means to me? It's where my mom spent some of her last day. She stole my memories of it for years. All it does is remind me of what I've lost.

"Please? Could we maybe go outside in the yard if we need more space?" I can't help the pleading tone, the desperation.

She's already forcing me to be around Ash every day. I can't do this, too.

She sighs, setting a comforting hand on my shoulder. "It's this important to you?"

I breathe in relief. She's listening to me. "Yes. Yes, Grandma, it is."

"Okay. We can start in the backyard. But you can't avoid the shop forever, dear. It's part of who you are just as much as each of your limbs."

My body relaxes. "I would chop my own hand off if it gave me as much trouble as that shop."

"Mmm." Her nose wrinkles. "What lovely imagery."

"That's what I'm here for."

"Ever so charming. Now put a smile on, we have a customer."

CHAPTER 3

FIRST LESSON

Seven comes too quickly. I'm almost crawling out of my skin.

I want to learn magic, of course I do. But that first step is always the hardest and there's something life-altering about this. I know I won't be the same person—for better or worse—once I fully embrace my witchiness. I'm on the precipice of something important and I'm terrified I'll fall.

It makes me itchy. Irritated. Like I'll snap if someone looks at me wrong.

Grandma has spent the last hour outside preparing everything and I swear I can hear her talking to the ground. Which, logically, isn't that far outside the realm of possibility, since she's an Earth witch.

But still.

"Ready?" Hazel asks, as she comes up beside me.

She's so different now that she's found Noah and isn't living under the constant cloud of our mother. Confident, happy, unburdened. It's hard not to take on the responsibility of knowing that she would've always been this way if not for me and Mom. Or maybe that's the regular-sex glow.

"Is Noah coming over tonight?" I ask instead of answering. He stays over at least a few times a week now that they made up a month ago. It's absolutely super adorable.

It's also strange.

We haven't had a man in the house since Dad. Emotion sticks in my throat like a thick wad of peanut butter whenever I think about it.

She nods. "Mhmm. He'll be over after our lesson. Is it okay that he comes over so often?"

I side-eye her. "You're expecting me to tell you not to see your soulmate regularly? To ban him from the house for no reason?"

Her hands fly up to grasp mine. "Of course not. But your comfort means a lot to me."

"Luckily I'm fine." I pull away. "Let's do this thing."

I turn from her guilt-ridden gaze and open the back doors. Dad fenced in the backyard when Hazel and I were kids to stop us from running off to God knows where. Now it's all lit up. Twinkle lights drape across the posts and create a small area with Grandma at the center.

There's a purple picnic blanket and three pillows where she stands. The flower garden twists and flourishes more than I've ever seen—especially in the winter—and the trees cast a bigger shadow.

It's freezing, but Grandma has lit a fire in the fire pit with what smells like a variety of herbs, creating a hazy, smoky glow.

It's beautiful.

"Wow, Grandma!" Hazel says, going down the back porch steps. "This is everything."

"If you pull out a muumuu for me to wear, I'm leaving." I step down as well, walking toward the pillows. Even with the blanket underneath them, the cold ground will seep through.

Thank God I wore my fleece-lined leggings.

A roll of Grandma's eyes is her only reply as she arranges us on the pillows as she likes. With me closest to the fire.

The warmth against my back is comforting, homey. It's my element. I knew when Hazel explained them for the first time. I just didn't want to admit it to her for some reason. Maybe because we're in such a weird place, maybe because I'm a secretive bitch. Either way, I haven't told either of them—and I have a feeling that's not going to cut it anymore.

Every witch has one element they connect to, that helps us harness our magic. Hazel told me she knew hers was air because something happened that was out of her control. I think it was a breeze or something.

"Today, we will connect with ourselves and our element. Return to the basics, so we can build from a solid foundation," Grandma says, her voice carrying across our space. "I am an Earth witch, Hazel is an Air witch. Laura, do you know your element?"

Fucking called it.

It makes sense that Grandma is tied to the earth, with her big, beautiful garden at her cottage and her grounding personality. And I've noticed that whenever Hazel gets upset, it almost feels like there's a small tornado whipping around until she calms down. And Mom—her connection to water was obvious the moment she disappeared in that liquid globe with Draven.

I take a deep breath as they both stare at me. "You know it's unsettling as fuck when you both just stare at me unblinking like that, right?"

Hazel cracks a small smile and I can't help returning it. Underneath it all, she's my sister.

"You didn't answer the question," Grandma sasses. Rosie—her ancient black cat—trots over from the porch and plops into Grandma's lap. I didn't even notice the little feline was outside. She's been accompanying Grandma when she stays over and it's nice having an animal in the house.

Mom never allowed pets.

"Fire."

Hazel's eyes light up like she's a kid on Christmas morning. "Really? Fire? That's so cool. How did you find out?"

Do I lie or do I tell the truth? Do I tell them that fire has been whispering unintelligible nonsense to me since I got my first period at ten? Or do I make up some oh-I-set-something-on-fire-once-whoops excuse?

They're staring at me again.

"Does it matter? I don't know how to control it and that's what we're here for," I say instead. Not a lie, but also get-the-fuck-out-of-my-face enough to hopefully get them to drop it.

Hazel's eyes dim as she settles back onto her pillow. I don't really want to push her away, it's just subconscious at this point. I don't know how to ask for what I need from her to rebuild our relationship. I don't have the words.

"I suppose you're correct, if not a little bit rude about it," Grandma says, frowning at me. "Lessons are about connecting with—and harnessing—your magic and control. Because your magic is as much a part of you as each of your toes."

"Interesting choice. Got a thing about feet?" I needle her.

"If I did, it would not be about your gnarled claws."

A laugh bursts from me just as the fire crackles and pops. "Nice!"

"Oh, you two are impossible." The corners of Hazel's mouth turn up despite the words.

Rosie *mews*, batting her paw against Grandma's arm in what looks like utter frustration.

"Right you are, Rosie dear. Getting back on track, we start with meditation," Grandma continues, closing her eyes. She crosses her legs and settles onto the pillow, relaxing her body.

"You don't have to close your eyes, but you do need to focus on relaxing and listening." Grandma places her hands on the patch of ground purposefully left uncovered by the blanket, despite the cold. "Feel your body, feel every connection point. Where your hands touch, where your legs touch. We'll start at the top of our heads today."

Slowly, she has us tense and relax each muscle; it's not long until I'm in a sort of trance. The air is thick and smoky, the fire crackling.

Whispering.

What are you saying to me? What do you want me to know?

I'm dry. Parched to the point of feeling like my skin will flake off in grains of sand.

Everything is hot.

Hot, hot, hot. And I can't see. Can't hear.

Only feel. Feel the lack of water and the heat. It's so hot.

I don't want to be here. I want to go home.

"Laura!" The call is jarring. "Laura!"

Hands are on my arms, shaking my body until I open my eyes to the backyard. To Grandma and Hazel. To the crackle and pop of the fire and the light of the stars in the sky.

"Laura, you were screaming," Hazel murmurs, gathering me in her arms. For the first time in a long while, I don't push her away. I burrow into her chest, into the refuge she provides.

"What did you see?" Grandma asks. I don't like her worried tone.

How do I explain it? I don't even know what I saw. How I did that.

I shake my head.

What just happened to me?

CHAPTER 4

PERFECTLY FINE

I lock my bedroom door and don't emerge until the next morning. Every time I close my eyes, the overwhelming memory of the heat threatens to take me under again.

I don't sleep much.

Bags under my eyes have never been a thing, not on *this* face. Not with my perfected skin care routine. But today they are real and I hate it. Is this how normal people feel all the time?

Normal people. Messing around with magic only reminds me how absolutely not normal I am, no matter how much I pretended to be.

I never let people too close, though. My 'friends' stopped asking about me after I skipped two outings, and any guys I may have been talking to fell off as well.

What are they doing right now? Probably sleeping off a wicked hangover from a night of bar hopping, flirting, and dancing as if they didn't have a care in the world.

I don't miss the people. But I miss pretending I didn't have a care in the world.

I throw on a chunky, distressed cream sweater and thick fleece-lined leggings with knee-high winter boots, and so much concealer I will probably look like a creasy weirdo in a couple hours. Oh well. No one cares what I look like anymore, anyway.

"Hey." Hazel stops me from leaving the house with a hand on my arm. Noah leans on the banister behind her, shooting me a cautious smile. Noah is all tall, lanky, lean lines. At somewhere over six foot, he makes Hazel look more like a pixie than a witch. He and I still don't really know each other, despite him apparently being my family now. But from what I've gathered, he's incredibly sweet and incredibly nerdy. "Are you okay?"

I sigh. "I didn't put on enough concealer, did I?"

She smiles, the worry still poking through. "You look beautiful, as always. But I was there last night. I heard you screaming."

All I could feel, see, or hear was heat. I had no idea I was screaming until Hazel said it last night.

And the dehydration. I drank about three bottles of water last night.

"I'm fine." I plaster on an I'm-entirely-normal smile. "It was nothing."

It was obviously not nothing, and the skeptical glance I'm getting in response proves that she's aware of it, too. But until I know what happened, there's nothing I can say to make her, or myself, feel better.

"We'll talk about it in the car." Grandma comes up to us with a sympathetic smile on her weathered face. "But we'll be late if we don't go now."

I nod and follow Grandma, leaving Hazel's worry behind in the creaking house. Leaving both of them behind.

It's quiet as Grandma and I get in the car, both of us lost to our thoughts.

Hazel, as always, knows exactly how she feels about everything the second it happens. Me? I need a second to process shit. And whatever the fuck happened last night is a lot to figure out.

I think I'm scared. I think I'm no longer convinced I'm not crazy. Hearing voices is never a good sign, it can't be.

"You are processing what happened last night and you don't

have the words to describe it yet. Am I correct?" Grandma asks from the driver's side, after we've been driving for a few minutes.

"Uh . . . yeah, that's pretty much it," I reply. I'd rather she believe that than let her know I'm contemplating my sanity.

She nods. "I would assume so. You've probably never had something like that happen to you."

"What was it?" I ask, knowing she probably won't have the answer. It happened in my own head, after all.

She glances at me, tightening her hands on the wheel. "Could be any number of things. Spirits, connection to a memory, a message. But despite how you reacted, it may not have been bad. It's hard to say."

May not have been bad? It definitely sucked. I'm glad she's not pressuring me, though. She's just letting me do my own thing.

"That being said, it may happen again as we train. And I want you to be prepared for that possibility."

I groan.

"How are you otherwise, dear?"

She's trying to keep up a conversation today and part of me appreciates that she cares, but part of me misses the silence of yesterday. I used to hate the quiet. I would always be the one to fill it with nonsense. Now? I don't really have that much to say.

At least, I don't have much to say to Grandma and Hazel.

"I'm fine," I reply after a beat. "Perfectly fine."

She sighs. "As we all are."

I can't keep talking about this. I flip my hair over my shoulder, putting on the mask I'm so used to wearing. "How did you find out you were an Earth witch?"

"Mm." She turns in to the market. "I was raised differently than you and Hazel. My parents were very invested in our bloodline and in our magic, so I was taught how to look out for manifestations from the very beginning. I learned how to test each element, to reach out to each of them and see if they speak to me."

Like the way fire speaks to me?

A wistful smile blooms on her face, softening the lines etched on her skin and making the years fall away. "One day I was sitting in my mother's garden and I wished her prized red rose bush had no thorns. Each one of them fell off in an instant."

My mind twirls around her words as we park and walk toward the market. I have so many questions but I don't know how to ask any of them. So am I the only one fire speaks to? Does magic work that way? Is something wrong with me? How differently would our lives have gone if Mom nurtured our magic the way Grandma's parents did?

"Are you going to stay today?" I ask as we approach our booth. Someone to play interference with Ash, even someone as meddling as Grandma, would be lovely.

She raises an eyebrow. "Do you need me to?"

She's challenging me. And damn it, I'm not a little girl who needs to be coddled.

I shake my head, blonde ponytail moving with it. "Nope. It's not like it's hard. I just figured you'd want a break from Hazel."

"It's Wednesday. Though she doesn't teach classes anymore, this is her day off. If you needed me, I'd have just kept the shop closed, but since you don't . . ." Her eyes twinkle with mischief. The old schemer.

"Guess I'll be just fine." I fake a grin, my eyes already involuntarily moving toward where Ash's booth usually sits. I don't see any large, lumbering oafs, though. Which is odd.

"Looking for someone?" She asks, false innocence in her tone.

"Who would I be looking for, Grandma?" If she and Hazel are talking about Ash behind my back, too, I swear to God I will throw someone down a flight of stairs.

Even if it's myself.

"I may have seen you speaking to a certain woodworker when I was with my friends yesterday. I don't plan on mentioning him to anyone, though. I am also not going to mention that he usually doesn't have his booth up on Wednesdays since he drives his father to his appointments."

"Appointments?" The question is out of my mouth before I can stop it. I don't want to know more things about him. Keeping him at arm's length is hard enough as it is.

She nods sadly. "Ash's father, Birch—"

"BIRCH?"

"Good to know your ears are working, dear. As I was saying —" She cuts me a glare full more of fondness than anger. "Ash's father, Birch, used to own the woodworking business. Had done ever since his father passed it down to him—"

"What was his father's name? Spruce? Oak? Douglas?"

"Up until about a year ago when he was diagnosed with cancer," she continues as if I said nothing. "Ash was his apprentice at the time, but took over the majority of the business so Birch could focus on treatments."

"That's a lot to deal with," I reply, my chest aching at the thought.

My father died quickly and unexpectedly. One day he was there and the next he wasn't. What would it be like if I had been forced to watch him slowly wither away?

I'm not sure which I would prefer.

She nods once. "Birch is a good man. I met him when he was a teenager. He and your mom didn't really run in the same circles, but they did hang out in big groups together once or twice."

That's a mindfuck if I've ever heard one. Mom as a teenager hanging out with my future soulmate's dad.

My gaze lingers on the empty space where Ash usually stands. Would I have ever known any of this if Grandma hadn't told me?

"Well." She gives my shoulder a gentle pat full of affection. "I'm going to head out. Call me if you have any questions!"

And with that—and the clickity-clack of her millions of bangles—she leaves me by myself.

It's lonelier than I expect.

CHAPTER 5
A TENT

Manning the booth went better than I thought it would —not that I had high expectations to begin with. I made a few sales and, when I took a small break, found a woman who makes artisan soaps infused with magic. Overall, a good day. Since Wednesday went so well, I feel more confident as I stroll into the market the next day.

And then I see Ash.

Putting a tent up over my table like he owns the damn place.

I stomp over and glare at him. "What exactly do you think you're doing?"

"Exactly what it looks like, Goldilocks." He turns from his handiwork, grinning at me with all the self-satisfied glee in the world. "Putting up a tent."

"Thank you, genius, I can see that. I meant, what are you doing putting up a tent around my booth when no one asked you to? For no apparent reason?"

"It's supposed to snow today. I didn't want all your merchandise getting ruined so I got here early with *two* tents—one for you, and one for me."

The pure kindness of the act threatens to steal the breath from my lungs. He may have ulterior motives. He may be using this as an excuse to see me, as an excuse to talk to me, as an excuse to continue this antagonistic-but-somehow-mostly-playful banter we've got going on.

But the look in those emerald-green eyes says he genuinely cares and wants me protected. Happy.

It rips at the part of me that feels so goddamn lonely I can barely stand it. Fuck, Ash, why do you have to make it so difficult to protect you? I can't let you get hurt, too.

I pick at the white fabric. "No one asked you to do this. What if I had brought my own tent?"

He shrugs, grin falling just a tad, which makes my chest hurt. "I don't see one, so I think that's a moot point."

"Surprised you know what that word means."

"Gigantic brute school is very thorough when it comes to vocabulary."

"Apparently." I'm taken aback by how easy it is to banter with him. How fun. "Well, if you're all done then, can you leave? I don't want you scaring away potential customers."

"I don't know," he says, voice dripping with sex and good God it's attractive. "I think I deserve a thank you for my hard work."

I cross my arms, his eyes following the movement. The hunger in them causes my body to tremble. "I'm deciding not to call this vandalism and report you to whomever oversees this outfit. That's your thank you."

"May I request a different kind of thank you?" His voice lowers, the moment of lost confidence nowhere to be seen.

I inhale sharply. "You may, but that doesn't mean I'll agree to it."

"That's fair." He comes in close, but not touching. Never touching. I get the feeling that's the line he won't cross. Not until I tell him to. The thought makes me shiver. "Come with me somewhere tomorrow morning."

I scoff, even though the idea of going anywhere with Ash

Cedar causes an unwelcome frisson of glee to slide up my spine. "Does that usually work? No details, no real plan? Just 'come with me'?"

"Work in what way?" His half smile curves up on one side, and suddenly I want that beard scratching every inch of me. "Are you implying something untoward?"

A cool breeze stirs the tent, bringing with it the scent of snow. And him.

Instead of answering, I glare at him. Maybe if I turn mute suddenly he'll think I'm insane and simply go away.

"So, whaddya say, Goldilocks?" He smirks and gives me a nonchalant shrug. "I mean, I can always take the tent back down."

"You wouldn't dare."

The cocky expression on his face says he absolutely would. I heave a giant breath and throw my hands in the air. "Fine! I'll accompany you to whatever utterly archaic activity you have planned to say thank you for doing something no one asked you to do."

He shifts, drawing attention to the strain of his shirt across his chest. His presence is overwhelming. I need to get him away from me before I do something ridiculous like hit him for being so attractive.

Or worse. Kiss him.

"I'll need your phone number. So I can come and get you in the morning."

"Absolutely not!" I shake my head and step back. "Why don't you just tell me when and where to be, and I'll show up bright-eyed and bushy-tailed?"

"Because I'm not an idiot. I do that, you won't show up." He chuckles, obnoxiously warm and bubbly and bright. "Give me your phone or I'll stand here all goddamn day bothering your customers until you do."

Fuck you, you giant monster.

I hesitate for a beat—two—before I finally give in. Seems I can't say no to him as easily as I like to think.

As I hand him my phone, I can't shake the feeling that I'm making both the biggest mistake of my life and the best decision I've ever made.

CHAPTER 6
NO ONE LIKES A KISS-ASS

Ash is right about it snowing today, and that puts me in a pissy mood. Not the snow itself—for a Fire witch I'm actually quite fond of snow.

No, I'm just pissed off he was right about something.

The hulking brute.

He does, however, stay away from my booth after he gets my phone number, which is both a blessing and a curse. Being so close to him is weakening my defenses.

I step into my old Victorian home at the end of the day with exhaustion weighing me down. I practically collapse on the carpet in the foyer.

Until I smell lasagna.

The best thing about Noah? His Nonna Ricci. I've never met her myself, but he frequently brings her food to the house—and Lord Almighty that woman is a saint. Blessed by the heavens to be the best cook in the world.

Which I would never mention in Grandma's presence.

I follow my nose to the kitchen to find Noah draped around Hazel's back, kissing her neck as she pretends to wave him off.

A pang of jealousy rises up to catch in my throat. Hazel has everything now. I don't even recognize us anymore.

She has a soulmate she's entirely unafraid of being in a relationship with, despite the overwhelming evidence she's being dumb as fuck for having him in her life. She has a passion she's making a business out of.

Just looking at her is a reminder of everything I don't have. Including a good relationship with her.

"Can you two unglue yourselves for five minutes so I can get to the plates? I'm fucking starving," I say, hand on my hip. Deflecting my emotions with borderline bitchy humor. How on brand for me.

Despite my words, Noah just smiles at me and leans his chin on top of Hazel's head. "Plates are right there."

How dare he not find me scary. I am bitch, hear me roar.

"Want to watch a movie while we eat? Might be a nice way to relax before training," Hazel says, watching as I plate up dinner.

Sisterly bonding, how fun. As if I'm not still salty as fuck over her telling me her life with me was nothing. She was unconscious for days after that stupid fucking daemon attack and when she woke up, something changed in her. She finally told me exactly how she felt about me, after years of hiding behind a filter.

I only held her back. Everything she'd done for me meant nothing to her.

I left with her dried blood still lingering under my fingernails.

We haven't processed that conversation or the fallout that followed, and I'm very much not ready to do so. Although a movie doesn't require conversation, and do I really want to sit in my bedroom by myself?

Again?

Like I do every night?

"Fine, but if the movie sucks, I'm leaving."

~

"Laura, why don't you place a warming spell on the backyard?" Grandma asks. She set up the space in exactly the same way as she did for the first lesson while Hazel and I were finishing our movie, and this time there was no mention of setting foot in the shop. Thankfully.

I snort. "Right, because I know how to do that."

"The entire point is that you will learn. And we learn by doing. Come here." She holds her hand out to me, and I step forward to grab it. "Feel my magic reacting to yours. Take from my strength to strengthen yourself."

Mom touched each of us right before she . . . Is this what she was doing?

Whatever. I close my eyes and take a breath. Warmth floods my body, rippling and sliding along my skin like a warm blanket or a favorite fuzzy sweater. A smile slowly stretches across my face. The sensation would be unsettling if it weren't altogether comforting.

"Visualize," Grandma says. "See in your mind's eye what you want and manifest it."

"Oh, we're manifesting now, are we?" I snark.

"You would be if you would stop sassing me."

Hazel's snicker floats over from the porch.

As if I'm not already hyper-aware of what a failure at magic I am compared to Hazel. What a failure in everything. My anger flares to life, a bonfire blazing in my mind's eye. I imagine the space filling with magic, with pure heat.

Warmth builds in my chest; a glow grows and grows until it reaches the far edges of the backyard. I don't have to look, or check—I know I did it.

"Beautifully done, Laura. I had a feeling your magic would come naturally once you started lessons," Grandma says, pride evident on her face.

Maybe I'm not a complete failure after all.

"Laura has a lot of natural talent at pretty much everything she tries." Hazel approaches us, sitting on her pillow.

I roll my eyes. Does she even mean that? "No one likes a kiss-ass."

Her face falls. I guess she genuinely meant it, but God I just cannot hear anything out of her mouth without wanting to snap at her.

We need so much fucking therapy.

"I'm a little hesitant to try meditation today after what happened last time," Grandma admits as she and I join Hazel on our respective pillows.

The memory of the heat, the dehydration, tickles at my senses. I'd really rather not repeat that myself if possible.

"Instead." She claps her hands. "We are going to focus on summoning. Hazel, you will demonstrate how you can summon air in your hands. I will demonstrate how I summon earth. And we will have Laura make her first attempts at summoning fire."

This? This could be okay. No whispering magic, no unbearable heat. And fuck, I just did a pretty good job of heating the backyard. This will be a piece of cake.

"Sounds a lot more fun than making weird noises while sitting crisscross applesauce," I reply.

And feeling like I'm burning alive. Much more fun than that.

"Right." The look Grandma gives me is full of playful judgment, and I'll be the first to admit I deserve it. "Hazel?"

Hazel adjusts herself on her fluffy pillow. She carries herself differently ever since she met Noah, with more surety. She knows exactly who she is now. Like I used to.

With a flourish of her hands, she conjures a small tornado in her palm. It whips and turns in its own small area, not disturbing anything else.

It's cool. I guess.

"Wonderful, Hazel. Your speed with conjuring has improved significantly!"

I resist an eye roll.

Grandma lifts her hands in a similar motion, keeping one steady and one twirling above in a wave. Out of thin air, an orange poppy appears. The manifestation of the magic is a little different based on their elements, but the theory is the same. Create something where nothing existed before.

"Clear your mind and—" Grandma starts.

"Yeah, yeah, I got it." I don't need Grandma to tell me to connect to my element again. If anything, I'm too connected to the whispery fucker.

I lift my hands; the left is palm up and the right held above it, palm down. Nothing hard about it, just conjure fire out of literally nothing.

I close my eyes and listen to the crackle of the bonfire Grandma set just like last time. I am fire and fire is me, or something. Magic slips down my spine, running along my body like a comforting hand.

"Laura, that's beautiful." Hazel's gasping breath makes me open my eyes.

Between my hands is a twisting blue flame. It licks at my right hand but doesn't burn. It *is* kind of beautiful, actually. The way it undulates almost looks like it's dancing, beckoning me closer.

I gaze at the fire, and there they are. The little indistinct whispers I always hear. Sometimes they're quiet, sometimes they're louder, but they're always gibberish. Except when someone asks about the funeral.

About Mom.

I'm back in the heat. That sweltering, overwhelming chasm of darkness. I don't see anything but the flame in front of me, don't hear anything but the crackling roar of the fire.

Help.

HELP!

"Laura, come back now!" Grandma's voice is far away, like she's at the end of a long tunnel. I follow it. Just her voice, until I can feel her fingers on my temples and see the fear in her eyes.

The heat fades away.

~

IT TAKES a few moments for the last vestiges of smoke to clear from my mind, for me to feel safe. And even when I'm finally convinced I'm not in the heat anymore, I don't really feel that safe.

"What the hell is happening?" Hazel murmurs.

"Laura has to be ready to tell us," Grandma replies. "And that will only happen on her own time."

She's being surprisingly nonchalant about this entire thing, and I'm not sure if that makes me feel better or worse. She'd be full-on panicking if it were really bad, right?

"You both are under the impression I know what's happening." I meet their stares. Hazel looks back with frustration and Grandma with barely restrained amusement.

I'm glad one of us is having a good time.

"Maybe if you talk us through it, we can help you figure it out." Hazel scootches a little closer, her green eyes lighting up. "We're stronger together."

"Are we?" I snort. "I'm pretty sure nobody here but Grandma knows what they're actually doing."

Grandma lifts a hand. "Are you ready to tell us, Laura, or would you like to end our lesson here for the evening?"

Am I ready to tell them? For some reason, it feels like I'm opening up to them in a way I haven't before. I'm not a super vulnerable person in general, but telling them about the visions—if that's even what they are—will lead to telling them about the whispering.

And the whispering is mine.

I shake my head, pointedly not looking in Hazel's direction. I don't want to see the disappointment in her face, or the rejection.

This isn't about her.

I stand and walk back inside, determined not to feel guilty about doing what feels right to me.

"I have cheesecake." Noah's voice comes from the left and I swear I jump seven feet out of my skin.

My hand flies to my chest. "Fuck, we need to get you a bell or something!"

His smile is almost infectious. He's too happy—it should annoy me, but it doesn't for some reason. "I was thinking about getting Rosie one, maybe I'll get one for myself, too."

"Good." I walk toward the kitchen. "Where's the cheesecake?"

We plate it up in silence. Hazel and Grandma haven't come inside yet. They're probably discussing me again. They love to plot.

Well, they can plot and be shady, and I'll enjoy cheesecake.

"Noah, how does it feel to be the only normal guy in a family of witches?" I ask. It's got to be an interesting dynamic . . . More entertaining than any trashy reality TV show, that's for sure.

"I can't pretend it was an easy thing to come to terms with. You saw how I reacted." The guilt is written clear across his face.

I swallow a bite. Oof, this woman has to be a witch. "You reacted that way because of the lying, not the magic. At least that's how I heard it."

"That's a fair point, but I would be lying if I didn't admit that the magic tripped me out, too. It's a lot to swallow. But a nerd finding out that there's magic in this world? I'm definitely cool with it."

"Yeah, I guess magic would be kind of your dream, huh?"

He shrugs. "Hazel is my dream. The magic is just fun."

He's so open with his affection when it comes to my sister, even when she's not in the room. It's easy. No games or manipulation.

He just loves her. My heart throbs at the purity of it. At how easy it is for them to love each other.

"And the soulmate thing?" I'm not sure why I'm even asking him, to be honest. Not like I have a soulmate I'm avoiding but somehow spending time with tomorrow morning on a not-date.

Couldn't be me.

He smiles. "It's pretty awesome, to be honest. But that might be because it's Hazel. She's my future."

"You really don't mind the whole constant danger thing?"

"Nothing is for certain." He makes deliberate eye contact with me. "Nothing is a given. And I would rather spend a few days with her than a lifetime without her."

Goosebumps raise along my arms at the seriousness in his tone. At the pure love in his voice. The devotion.

It sounds a lot like the few memories I have of Dad with Mom.

"Did you know something was different with her? Even before she told you what you were to each other?"

"Oh yeah. It was obvious." His eyes trail to the window, lighting up when they find her outside. "I knew the second I laid eyes on her that she was different. I thought it was weird at first, how quickly we connected. I even asked her if she'd ever felt anything like this. But that soulmate bond goes both ways. I want her just as much as she wants me."

Does Ash want me just as much as I want him? In my determination to keep him safe, I may have ignored how he is feeling. Noah is making me realize that pushing Ash away may be even harder than I thought.

He laughs. "Well, that's a face. Soulmate troubles?"

"Would you keep your voice down?" I practically whisper-screech. "Of course not. I don't have a soulmate."

His amusement is clear as he leans against the kitchen counter. "Of course not. It's definitely not a family thing that you all share."

I pout.

"I won't say anything to Hazel."

"Oh, bullshit!" I laugh. "You tell her everything. She just has to give you a look and you melt at her feet like an obedient puppy. You, sir, are the very definition of golden retriever vibes."

He shrugs. "I am what I am."

It's hard to be mad at a sunshine puppy. But I may have just spilled the beans about my soulmate problem to the one person I don't want to talk to about this.

Okay, the second. I don't want to talk to Ash or Hazel.

Or Grandma.
Or anyone.

CHAPTER 7

I WILL LIGHT YOU ON FIRE

W arm skin underneath my fingertips. Muscles shifting with each deliberate movement. Ash's scent in my nose as I cling to every second of sweet bliss.

RING RING.

My phone ringing pulls me out of an entirely too pleasant dream. My dreams are the only place I can have Ash—the only place I can be with him and keep him safe and pretend like everything is easy—and I may actually murder whoever ended that dream too quickly.

Where the fuck is my phone? I slap my hand around, finally finding it in the mass of blankets.

"What?" I growl. Who the fuck calls people anymore? Pretty sure my generation replaced that with text messages.

"I've dreamed about how your voice might sound when you just wake up, but goddamn do you put my best dreams to shame, Goldilocks," says the raspy voice that features in my dreams.

A blush travels up my cheeks and I thank God he can't see me.

"Ash, why are you calling me at—" I check the time "—FIVE A.M.?"

Frustration boils over. The man has a death wish.

His chuckle floats through the phone, all low and smoky. "You promised to come with me this morning, and I need your address."

"I did not promise a wake-up call before the sun comes up. Call me back in three hours."

"You promised to let me show you something, and that something won't be there in three hours. Text me your address or I'll keep calling every five minutes."

He'll do it, too. The fucking nag.

"Oh my God, fine!"

I expect he'll probably be here within the next thirty minutes, so there's no point trying to return to my much-needed beauty rest. If I look like a zombie, that's entirely his fault.

Butterflies erupt in my stomach at the thought of spending the morning with him. What will that be like?

I don't know how to feel about this.

With feline quietness, I dress and make myself a to-go cup of chocolate earl grey tea. I will absolutely need caffeine to function like a normal human, and I prefer tea to coffee.

Fight me.

So here I am, twenty minutes later, standing outside my house with my sparkly pink to-go cup, my winter boots and coat, and a thick woolen hat.

Our first snow of the year was decent. If I had to guess, we got about five inches—and it's still fluttering down in a soft cascade. The snowplows haven't been down our little street for a few hours, so everything is covered in an undisturbed blanket.

It's the perfect day to snuggle up with a cup of tea and a trashy TV show. But no.

As if the thought summoned him, a huge black pickup truck rumbles up to the house. 'Cedar Woodworking' is written on the side in big block lettering.

He jumps out, all chipper and happy. "Morning, Goldilocks!"

Even the winter-lumberjack porn—with his flannel, sherpa-lined jacket and heavy boots—doesn't make up for the fact that he's obviously a morning person.

I scowl.

"Are we compensating for something?" I ask, gesturing to the giant car.

"Want to find out?"

I roll my eyes. "That was horrible, even for you."

He just smiles at me, all sexy beard and handsomeness. "You're the one who brought it up. Let's get going."

Before I can get to the passenger-side door, he opens it and offers me a hand. To be fair, any normal person would need help getting into this thing, but I refuse to touch him. Instead, I scrabble and claw my way in, managing to climb inside with a relatively limited amount of embarrassment.

I don't meet his gaze. I don't want to see the smugness on his face at my struggle.

Noah's words play in my head as Ash gets in the other side.

I want her just as much as she wants me.

Does he really? How do I protect him if that's the case?

"You're pretty serious for this early," he remarks after a few moments of driving. I was so lost in my own head I hadn't even realized we were moving.

"I'm a serious person."

Lie. At least, I didn't used to be serious. I have no idea who I am now. Ash snorts as if he's thinking the same thing.

Silence falls like a blanket of snow over us again. It'd be so easy to ask him about his passion for woodworking, or what the small tattoo I just noticed on the inside of his wrist means. But I don't want to keep opening the door further whenever he asks. I shouldn't have agreed to this little journey, even if he did threaten to take the tent away. Who needs a tent, anyway?

I turn to the window, watching the wintery morning pass by.

I should've told Grandma to stuff it when she made me man the booth. What was that old crone going to do? Beat me to death with her walking stick? Set her elderly cat on me?

I'm in a fucking hole of my own making.

"We're here," Ash says, turning the car off.

I turn to face him and . . . he's right there. Every inch of him. This close, I can't pretend he's not the most brutally handsome man I've ever seen. A light beard covers a superhero chin and full lips. His nose is straight, leading up to shining emerald eyes draped in long black lashes.

I think I could stare at him for the rest of my life and never get bored. I could always find something new to focus on, to learn about.

A smile curves the top of his mouth on one side. On anyone else it would be cocky, and maybe it is a little bit, but there's an underlying care there. "Fuck, if you could see the way you look at me."

My heart stutters at his tone.

"It's probably good I can't," I huff, pulling back. "Watching other people gag makes me want to throw up."

He opens his mouth to reply and I lift my hand. "If you make a joke about gagging, I swear to God I will light you on fire."

His deep, rumbling laugh fills the car. "I wouldn't dream of it."

I slide out of the car before he can make it over to my side. We're in the middle of the woods—surprise to literally no one. His big lumberjack boots crunch on untouched snow as he carves a path through the trees. His hand is there, just waiting for me.

I don't take it.

I follow behind his broad shoulders, trying to ignore that even under the layers of shirt and sherpa-lined flannel I can see the muscles shift.

I'm obviously doing a great job of that.

"All right, Goldilocks." He turns abruptly and I barely refrain from slamming into him. "This is it."

I take a quick glance at the entirely nondescript area. Am I missing something? "We're in the middle of the woods, in the dark. Have you been horribly flirting with me all this time just to kill me?"

I don't think my soulmate would kill me. But, hey, you never know.

"You're here, so I don't think I've done that bad of a job." He winks.

I roll my eyes, crossing my arms.

When I don't reply, he steps closer. "Close your eyes."

If anything, I hold them open wider. "I'm good, thanks."

"You're lucky I like brats."

"And you're genuinely lucky I haven't set you on fire."

"That's the second time you've threatened to light me on fire." He cocks an eyebrow. "Fire witch?"

"None-of-your-business witch."

"Just come and look."

The sky is a blend of blues, pinks, oranges, reds, and yellows.

Sunrise.

It makes the snow on the tops of the trees glow, reflecting the light back. Every second it changes just a little, some color overtaking the others as the sun rises beyond the horizon line and over the forest in front of us.

In moments, it's over.

"My father and I used to come out here in the morning on the weekends when I was learning the family business. We'd drink coffee, watch the sunrise, and then pick a new tree to fell," Ash says softly.

I stand in silence as he speaks. He's sharing a private, special place with me. He's being selfless and vulnerable with me in a way I'm not sure anyone ever has been.

And he does it with ease. With confidence. Despite how we bicker back and forth, how I push him away. He shows this to me with the confidence that in his most vulnerable moment I won't slash and wound him.

It's a trust I don't deserve.

Thoughts of my own father flood my mind. I don't think we ever watched the sunrise together. Would he have ever taken me somewhere like this? Was it in his plan to share sunrises together?

I guess it doesn't matter what he planned, because he's gone. Just like Mom. Hazel has Noah, Grandma has her entire community of friends and the shop. Who do I have?

A soulmate I can't bear to endanger.

No one.

"Hey," Ash says in that gentle voice. "You okay over there?"

"Yep. Just fine." *He* may be willing to expose his own vulnerabilities, but I'm not. I push a lock of hair behind my ear and change the subject. "Your father is sick?"

He nods, sunlight dappling the slightly lighter brown highlights in his beard. "Cancer."

"Is it bad?" I ask quietly. It doesn't seem right to speak louder than a whisper, to disturb this tentative truce we've acquired in the morning light.

"That's a hard question to answer." He rocks on his feet, a heavy breath escaping him. "It's cancer, right? So, it's not a great diagnosis. But we caught it early, so his doctors are optimistic."

I wipe furiously at my face, at the tears that escape. I know what it's like to lose a dad, but I don't know what it's like to have a sick one.

"He and I became a lot closer after my mom left. I barely remember her, if I'm honest, and that's okay. I never felt like I was missing anything with him around."

I listen quietly, collecting these little pieces of him he gives freely.

"Shit." He scrubs his hands over his face. "I didn't mean to trauma dump on you. Especially knowing everything with your own dad and now your mom. I get talkative when I'm out here in the trees, among the woods and dirt."

"Mhmm. I'm not sure why you would tell *me*, though. All I've ever done is call you an overgrown brute."

His smile is big, genuine. "Oh, I'm sure you've thrown in some other flattering words."

"As if I could find flattering words to describe you."

The words have lost their bite a little bit. He sees through me in a way that makes me shiver in the cold Ohio morning.

I step back from him, from the view of the woods. "Should . . . Should we head back? The market will be starting soon."

His smile falls just a smidge, but the kindness never leaves his eyes. "Sure, Goldilocks. Can't have you being late."

CHAPTER 8
BELLE

By the time next Thursday at the market rolls around, I've successfully avoided both Ash and Hazel and got through a couple magic lessons without going all witchy-fire-coma.

All in all, a good week.

Grandma doesn't push me, so she gets to stay. Although to be fair, she spends most of her time in her shop, and whenever she's at the market she's gossiping with her old biddies.

"Sabrina said that Marsha said that Jan was seen out with Eddie Harper," one of the biddies loudly whispers over her tea. They've taken to using the tent as their own personal safe zone from the cold.

Grandma and the rest of the women gasp as I giggle. I can't say I don't enjoy it. They gossip like it's their job, and I am a sucker for old lady tea. Both literally and figuratively.

I've also gotten pretty decent at a warming spell, so the tent is comfortable despite the pillows of snow covering the ground. It's my way of bribing them not to gossip about me. I don't think it works that much.

"And you know Eddie was seen out just two weeks ago with Christine."

I stifle a laugh. They're incorrigible.

A light brush tickles my leg where I'm sitting at the booth and I jump. I bend in half under the tablecloth and there it is.

A cat . . . I think.

The creature's the size of a slightly bigger dog, but it's distinctly feline. One of those giant things you see on the internet that you can't believe is actually real and not in a zoo.

Big brown eyes blink up at me as I get out of my chair and drop to her level. She has golden fur with randomly placed dark spots.

Not that I've seen evidence that she is a she, but it's the vibe. I can just tell.

"Hi there," I coo softly. "Who are you?"

Big, rounded ears twitch at the sound of my voice. She gently pads a little closer.

"Do you belong to anyone? Do we need to find your people?" She doesn't have a collar, but that doesn't necessarily mean she's a stray. "Would you like to come out from under there?"

I back up a little, lifting the tablecloth up for her. She follows, getting up into my space. Her eyes lock with mine and with a delicate *mew*, she sits on my lap.

Well then.

"Looks to me like you've been adopted, dear," Grandma says, coming up behind me. I'm sitting on the ground with a ginormous cat in my lap. Totally normal.

"How do we know someone isn't looking for her?"

A gentle purr billows out of her chest as she nuzzles in.

Grandma pats my shoulder. "You can certainly make an effort, of course. But witches and cats have a long history. I fear you have a new companion for life."

"What do you think, cat? Do you want to come home with me?" I ask, scratching underneath her chin. Her purr intensifies, rumbling through my body. Not too dissimilar from the buzz of the soulmate bond, if I'm honest.

"You didn't have a choice in the matter!" one of the biddies says from where they're watching me.

I don't suppose I do.

After a walk through the market to truly make sure no one recognizes her, I gather Cat up and take her to the pet store before taking her home. Thankfully Grandma already has some things for Rosie, but Cat will need her own things.

I push the door to our house open, Cat still bundled in my arms.

I also need to come up with a name for her other than Cat. That's terrible.

"What do you think? Do you have any name suggestions?" I ask Cat as she chows down on her dinner.

She doesn't spare me a look. Fair.

I'm on my own, it seems.

I watch her eat as I sit on my bed. Apparently witches and cats have a *thing*, so maybe my witchy powers can tell me what her name is.

Her tail swishes back and forth, long legs ready to pounce at a moment's notice. She probably needs a bell just like Noah and Rosie.

I snort.

Belle.

"What do you think about the name 'Belle?'" I ask her.

She lifts her head slowly from her food, making eye contact with me once again. She huffs, gives a slight nod, and then goes back to eating.

Guess her name is Belle.

CHAPTER 9

A WEIRDO AMONG WEIRDOS

"Tonight, we conjure our element outside of our hands. We connect with and create our element outside of our inner circle," Grandma announces. We're in the backyard yet again a full week later.

She'd been taking it easy on me in magical lessons, trying not to push another magical episode, but I had a feeling there was an expiration date on her kindness.

Rosie and Belle wait on the porch, watching us intently. They don't love each other, but they're able to exist together. Based on Noah's shocked reaction, I expect it's a magic thing.

He's practically jumping from the kitchen window wanting to pet them, but Hazel insists he stays inside during magic lessons, just in case any stray magic hits him. It's a fair rule.

"Hazel, will you demonstrate?" Grandma continues, taking a step back from my sister. Allowing her space to work, probably, and I follow suit.

Logically, I understand why Grandma wants Hazel to demonstrate. Hazel knows what she's doing, unlike me. But I've grasped things relatively quickly, I don't need them to keep babying me.

"Get it, baby!" Noah calls from the open window. Hazel giggles, blowing him a kiss.

They are both ridiculously dorky and adorable, and it makes me want to roll into a ball and hide.

I've managed to continue avoiding Ash by a very graceful bob-and-weave method. Anytime I feel his approach, I hide. And he hasn't texted. But I know there's an expiration date on that, too. I'm not sure how to talk to him after our sunrise together. Being mean just seems cruel, but it's easier in the long run.

Better to reject him now before I break his heart. Or he breaks mine.

Hurting each other is inevitable. Even with Mr. and Mrs. Perfect standing here in front of me, I know they're on a timer, just as much as Mom and Dad were. I'm just trying to follow the path with the least amount of pain.

Hazel's deep breath pulls me back to the present.

She closes her eyes and waves her hands in front of her. As if she could create a breeze simply with the movement. She murmurs a little to herself and then throws her hands forward. A small tornado, maybe four feet tall, springs up a few feet away. It whips and gnashes at the air around it, but doesn't pull anything else to it.

If I wasn't seeing the damn thing in front of me, I wouldn't believe it existed.

"Excellent, Hazel!" Grandma praises, clapping her hands. "You've come so far!"

I roll my eyes. Gotta love that favoritism.

Hazel always got all the attention. I may have gotten it from the outside world because I demanded it, but she got it at home. Mom always fought with her, Grandma always enjoyed talking with her.

There was never much left for me.

"Laura, would you like to try?" Grandma asks kindly. She doesn't show disbelief or rudeness, but I can't view it as anything other than a challenge.

Can I do what Hazel does? Can I be as good as her?

I absolutely can.

I have to.

Closing my eyes, I block out the overwhelming presence of my family. I focus on my breathing instead, relaxing my body like Grandma taught me to. My connection to fire has always been there, always been such a strange little part of my life. I can tap into it.

I think about conjuring with fire, about creating a small ball of fire to hover in the same spot Hazel placed her tornado.

I open my eyes and find the smallest flicker of blue flame. It stands all alone, dancing in the air.

"Beautifully done, dear," Grandma says, hand on my shoulder. "Your powers are growing quickly."

The fire flickers at the praise, as if it's proud of us for what we've created. It's not a tornado, but it's mine.

Help.

A whisper on the air. A small plea I would've ignored if not for the general stillness of the outdoors.

Help.

It whispers again. It's soft, pleading, drawing me in.

"I don't know how to help you," I reply, with more eagerness than I expected. As strange as this is—as terrifying as the heat is—I'm a little excited. I want to know more. "I don't know what you need. I don't know who you are."

"What was that?" Grandma asks, not removing her hand from my shoulder.

I shake my head. Too many voices at once. "The fire said it needs help."

"The . . . fire?" Hazel asks. I can feel her skepticism from here, it's practically bleeding off her. "What do you mean?"

And that's exactly why I didn't want to tell her.

"I mean what I said," I huff. "I'm not speaking another language. The fire said 'help.'"

"Even in our world, it is unique for our elements to speak to us. Especially using language," Grandma explains.

Huh. So I'm a weirdo among weirdos. Cool.

"Do you think maybe since Mom died—" Hazel starts.

"She is not dead!" I practically screech at the same time as the fire blazes, snapping at my family with the same ferocity. We react as one. And something about it feels damn good. Validating.

Something believes me. Something doesn't pity me.

I don't look at Grandma and Hazel. I don't want the 'honey, you're just traumatized' response that I know is coming.

I know I'm traumatized, but I also know that something is going on. The fire is against me giving up on Mom—and despite that woman giving up on me every single day before her disappearance, I'm not getting talked out of this.

I turn on my heel and stalk into the house, Belle hot on my trail.

I may be the only one who hears their element, but I'm not going to be the only one who listens. I'm going to find some way to convince those two idiots that something more is going on.

CHAPTER 10
BULLSHIT

"I don't think I've ever seen you this angry, other than when you're talking to me. Should I be jealous?" Ash's amused voice startles me out of glaring at nothing the next day.

He never sneaks up on me. I must be more distracted than I thought.

Belle *mrows* at him from where she's twisted around my legs, pulling his attention away from any response I may have had for him.

She stands, stretching lazily, and approaches where he crouches down in a squat.

I can't see what his ass looks like in that position—thank God—but his thighs are thick and muscled and sinful.

"And who is this darling?" he asks, holding his hand out for her to sniff.

Here I was thinking she was an angel, but she's already snuggling up to the enemy. Traitor.

Am I jealous of a cat now? Fuck this.

"I've missed you," he adds quietly. It's a soft, honest admission that shoots through my chest like a painful lance.

"Her name is Belle," I reply, ignoring his confession.

After yesterday's incident with the fire, I barely have the energy for Ash Cedar. I don't have the energy to verbally spar with him or to pretend I don't dream about riding him until I'm screaming every night.

His hand is definitely not wrapped around my neck, either.

"Hi Belle," he coos at her. "Aren't you beautiful?"

"Don't tell me you're a cat person."

He meets my gaze. "I'm an Earth witch, Goldilocks. I'm an everything person."

While he hasn't outright said he's an Earth witch before now, it's the only thing that would make any sort of sense. The whole family-business-of-trees thing and connection to the earth is like a neon fucking sign.

I cross my arms and barely refrain from sticking my tongue out at him. It absolutely doesn't warm my heart or make my insides tingle that Belle adores him so much.

They're also very not cute together.

Whatever.

"What's got you all worked up?" Ash asks, fully sitting on the cold ground now as Belle nuzzles into his neck.

Lucky bitch.

"I'm not worked up." Even as I say it, I cringe. I sound like I have a stick so far up my own ass I could choke on it.

The eyebrow raise I get in reply proves it.

"Fine!" I throw my hands up. "There's just weird shit in my family ever since my mom . . . whatever. And weird shit with my magic."

He slides his thick fingers over Belle's ears, her purr so loud I can hear her from where I sit. "I'll be the first to admit I'm not the best at mom dynamics, seeing as it's only ever been me and my dad. But I can help with magic shit."

The words 'it's none of your fucking business' are on the tip of my tongue, but I can't force them out. How nice would it be to have someone else to talk to about this whole witchy nonsense?

Talking to Hazel is a goddamn minefield, and Grandma is great, but I don't trust her not to be plotting with my sister.

"I'm a Fire witch," I say, unable to stop a little bit of pride from leaking out.

He nods with a knowing smile. "Had a feeling. What's going on with it that's got you weirded out?"

"Fire whispers to me." Maybe this was the trick all along. Tell him that fire talks to me and convince him I'm insane.

I bet he'll keep his distance now.

"Okay." His eyebrows knit together and it makes me want to smooth the lines out with my thumb. "Elaborate for me."

I huff a breath. "I don't know. It's just always been a thing. I don't fucking understand it! It's just that when I focus on the flames, I can hear whispers. They don't ever mean anything to me, it's all gibberish. Except for recently. Hazel wants to have a funeral for Mom—for, like, closure or whatever—and every single time she brings it up, the fire says no. And I've been keeping it to myself because Hazel's a judgy bitch, and I let it slip finally last night."

"That's definitely weird. But I think you're right to want to take some time to figure out what that means for you," he says. Easily. As if it's the most obvious thing in the world. As if he just understands where I'm coming from.

Just gets it.

What the fuck.

"Can you go back to being an unreasonable brute, please?" I ask, a small smile creeping across my face. "This whole understanding bit is getting weirder than the whispers."

His laugh is loud, unrestrained joy that I want to roll around in. Soak in. Enjoy. "I promise not to be too helpful."

"That's not a hard promise to make for you."

"I don't know, Goldilocks, everyone else seems to find me helpful. You seem to be the only one who doesn't like me."

His words stop me short. Of course I like him.

The entire problem is that I like him.

He's funny, witty, intelligent, hardworking, selfless with his family, has the body of a god, and talks to me like I'm an intelligent peer. Not an idiot or a child.

And I can't fucking have him.

Frustration burns in my chest until it hurts. Why can't I just not give a fuck like Hazel? She parades Noah around practically daring daemons to kidnap him—and he's a defenseless human!

At least Ash is a witch and could protect himself somewhat. But even that isn't good enough, and it makes no sense that I'm the only one who sees this.

"Hey." Ash pulls me out of my head. "I know you're worried about the whispering, but I can help you figure this out."

The kindness in his eyes, the understanding and softness in his voice, makes me want to cry.

The only person who wants to help me, and I can't even touch him.

I swallow the ball of emotion and turn my face into a blank mask. "I've got this. Thank you, though."

"Bullshit."

I grind my teeth. "Excuse me?"

He gently pushes Belle off his lap and stands. "I said bullshit."

"And what exactly do you think is bullshit?" I follow suit, standing to match him. I may not be a short woman, but his size dwarfs me completely.

That doesn't mean I'll back down, though.

"I get that you've got walls so high you can barely see past them, but at some point you're going to have to let someone in. And I'm telling you—showing you—that I want that person to be me. I'm showing up for you, Goldilocks."

Isn't that all I've ever wanted? For someone to show up for me? To choose me?

"Did you ever think that maybe I can open up, I just don't want to open up to you?"

The hurt that flashes across his face feels like a knife in my gut. Being mean will push him away, will protect him.

I have to protect him. He's dealing with enough, with his dad and trying to maintain his family business on his own.

"Bull." He steps closer. "Shit."

I square up to him, despite it hurting my neck to look up at him. "Stop saying that."

"Stop saying bullshitty lies, then."

"I'm not lying!"

I don't want him to leave me alone. I want to be selfish for five seconds and give in. I want to choose this man who chooses me, but I'm choosing to protect him. I'm choosing to be a better person than the shitty façade I show to everyone else.

I'm choosing to give him what he needs, even if it's not what he wants. Not what I want.

"I can feel how much you hurt." His voice drops so low I can barely hear him. "I can feel it in my fucking bones and I don't know why. But what I do know is that it means something."

My eyes burn at his tone, at the pleading in his voice.

I'm doing the right thing.

"Leave me alone," I whisper.

He nods, backing up a step. "Fine, I will. But I'm always here for you, despite how stubborn you can be. When you realize that, you know where I'll be."

And he leaves me alone with Belle glaring at me.

CHAPTER II
JUST LIKE YOUR MAMA

The house creaks and groans in welcome as I return home. My bones ache, my heart hurts, and I just want to curl up in bed with Belle for the next seventy-five years. Give or take a few.

Belle trails behind me up the stairs. I'd carry her myself, but honestly she's almost half the size of Hazel and I don't want her getting used to it.

We enter my room and a weight instantly lifts off my shoulders. My room is my only safe place in the world. It's pink—which started as an ironic joke, but everyone just assumed I was being serious that pink was my favorite color. The walls, the carpet, the sheets, my comforter. All pink. The only hints at my actual personality are in the small details.

The one framed photo of me and Hazel when we were children. Dad was a photographer, and he took the picture. I like to pretend I can remember him taking it when I look at it.

My janky, secondhand sewing machine. I know it's not allowed to be my dream anymore, I couldn't possibly go to Paris and design accessories. But I still stay up late sewing, even if it's just for me.

It's also covered in blankets.

One thing Hazel and I have in common is a love of fuzzy blankets.

Although I'm pretty sure she just indoctrinated me into the fuzzy blanket crew by force.

Before I'm even properly dressed down into my gray leggings and pink crop hoodie, Hazel barges into my room.

"Have you forgotten how to knock?" I ask, pulling the hoodie over my head. Belle *mrows* in solidarity. She's probably trying to earn back some of the affection she lost while snuggling with Ash.

Hazel sighs, some of the wind in her sails leaving her. "You're right. I shouldn't do that. I'm just fucking worried about you, and I haven't seen you since last night."

"While the concern is appreciated, it isn't necessary. You may leave."

I plop onto my bed, determined to win whatever staring contest Hazel started. If she wants to be stubborn, I can be more stubborn.

Just ask Ash.

"We have a lot we need to talk about. And I haven't pushed it because, honestly, we've both been through a lot the past couple months." She takes a cautious step further into the room. "But we can't avoid this anymore."

"Avoid what exactly?" There really should be a therapist present for this conversation.

"Can I come in?" she asks. She's already in the room, but I know what she's really asking. Can we address this weird tension between us? Can we start trying to fix this? Can we talk about Mom?

Why did she have to choose today? Today, when I had to force Ash away with tears blurring my vision.

I nod anyway. Maybe she's taking advantage of my emotional vulnerability, but I miss my sister.

She breathes a sigh of relief and sits on my bed, curling one of my blankets around her lap. "How are you after last night?"

"Honestly? I'm used to fire whispering to me, so it wasn't that big of a deal. The fact that it asked for help was more worrying than anything."

"You're used to it?" Her head cocks like a confused puppy's.

"It's been whispering to me since puberty. I've never been able to actually understand it, but I could understand that it was communicating." I slump against the headboard. I expected it to be strange, but it does feel a bit freeing to finally let out this huge secret.

She can't hide the shock on her face, her mouth forming a perfect 'o'.

"I didn't tell anyone because Dad was already gone at that point and Mom had banned magic. I knew if I mentioned it, I'd get in trouble and you and Mom would fight." I sigh. "So it became my secret."

"That makes sense." Her hand reaches for mine, grasping lightly. "I'm sorry you had to deal with that alone."

"You're making it sound like it was scary, or like I was worried. I knew it was magic and it was never threatening. It was almost fun. Something small that belonged to me."

"I can understand that. I'm sorry I initially didn't believe you. We've been through so much shit, I'm honestly surprised one of us hasn't had a mental break. I think I'm subconsciously waiting for it." She chuckles. It's a dry, humorless thing.

I match the sound. "Fair."

"I've missed you," she says quietly. "I'm sorry things got so messed up between us."

"I've missed you, too."

"I don't know what to tell you about the fire asking for help. I'm obviously not the person who has enough witchy knowledge to assist here. Grandma is probably the best place to start, and if not her, I'd suggest going to the shop and seeing if you can find anything in our family journals."

"Family journals?" It's my turn to cock my head.

She nods. "Our entire family history is documented all the

way back to Salem. I haven't read about any Fire witches yet, but it may be that another one had a similar experience."

I shudder at the thought of setting foot in the shop.

"Would you be willing to bring the journals home? So I can read them here?"

"You'd have to ask Grandma if she's okay with it, honestly. She doesn't like things being taken out of the shop for any length of time." She gives me a conspiratorial smile. "I think it's because she's a control freak."

"I'll ask her later."

Grandma's had a lot of patience for me lately, but all patience runs out eventually. And Hazel's not wrong about her being a control freak.

Belle *mews*, butting her head against Hazel's arm.

I chuckle. "Demanding everyone's attention just like your mama, aren't you?"

"She's beautiful, just like her mama."

We haven't talked about everything, but it's the first time I haven't felt scared to talk to my own sister. It's progress and I revel in it.

It would be silly to assume our relationship will go back to exactly the way it was. For better or worse, Hazel and I are different people than we were. And if we're going to fix things, we have to forge a way forward as the people we are now, not the people we were.

Ew, this is getting too sentimental.

"So, how's soulmate sex?"

"LAURA!"

～

I'M AVOIDING GRANDMA.

I need to ask her about the fire whispers, but she isn't up in my face about it and there's part of me that doesn't want to know. Part of me that's worried I'm some sort of freak.

Or that I'm evil.

Can kids absorb their parents' karma?

Okay, I can't keep going around and around in circles. Time to be a grown up and just do whatever it is I don't want to do. Like all other adults.

Grandma came with me to the market today, leaving Hazel alone in the shop, but she's not in my tent like usual. She's probably causing some sort of trouble.

A prickle of awareness raises the hairs on the back of my neck as I instinctively look to my left.

Ash.

We haven't spoken since our fight. He's probably trying to make a point that he's not going to push me until I'm ready to ask for help.

Joke's on him, though. I don't plan on ever asking him for help and I wanted him to stay away from me. So thanks, dude, but you're just shooting yourself in the foot.

"Making faces at people?" Grandma asks, sneaking up behind me like a ghost.

I grumble, breaking eye contact with Ash. "He deserves it."

"Of course, dear. He's a man." She winks. "He probably deserves worse."

I laugh, tension melting from my shoulders. God, I don't have enough fun anymore. I don't laugh enough anymore. "Can I ask you something, Grandma?"

"I don't know—can you?"

I glare at her. "How much do you know about Fire witches?"

"Not much, if I'm entirely honest. They're the rarest of the elemental witches. Forgive the pun, but they also tend to be the most fiery." She sits beside me at the booth. "Something you'd like to ask specifically about your magic?"

"The whispering," I admit, lowering my voice.

She gives me a guilty smile. "I don't know much about that, unfortunately. I vaguely remember seeing something about it in the family history, but I can't recall the specifics. May I suggest starting there?"

Pretty much exactly what Hazel said.

"Is there any way you'd be okay with Hazel bringing the family history book home so I can read there?"

She appraises me for a moment, eyes trailing over my face. "I don't love the idea of that book sitting forgotten in your room for months. But I'll allow it—"

"Thank you, Grandma!"

"—*if* you tell me why you don't want to go into the shop."

Fuck.

How do I explain this to her without ripping myself open?

"Too much has happened there," I reply. Let it go, Grandma.

She stares at me, her ocean-blue eyes searching me until I'm squirming. "Fine. You have a week with the book. Any longer and I'm coming into your room and getting it."

"Deal."

That's better than I was hoping for, so I'm not going to fuck that up by fighting with her.

CHAPTER 12
LONELY BEAUTY

If I had to guess, I'd say this book weighs exactly three million pounds.

The Women of The Pruitt Line. A comprehensive family tree with biographies of the Pruitt line all the way back to Salem.

The leather cover is decorated in flowers and embossed cursive text. It screams old, but considering these women were born four-hundred-plus years ago . . . Yeah, it's old.

The scent of magic—smoke, bonfire, and almost burned marshmallows—washes over me as I open it. The rightness of the moment settles heavily on me. Maybe magic is as much mine as it is Hazel's and Grandma's.

I flip through the pages. Of course, the witches aren't actually organized by anything other than timeline, so I'm looking for a fiery needle in a haystack. It may take some time.

Hazel has read a little bit so the pages don't stick, but they are stiff. This book deserves more love than it gets. Deserves to be seen, learned from. Read.

Frustration blooms in my chest. I would've been reading this as a fucking bedtime story if my magic hadn't been kept from me.

Is this how Hazel felt when she started learning her magic? I remember her being so angry, and I can't help feeling like I understand her a bit more.

My eyes lazily scan for the words 'fire' and 'flame,' but I'm not seeing much. Other than Elizabeth, the start of our line, being burned at the fucking stake.

Talk about yikes.

My thoughts stray to Ash, as they usually do when I'm not otherwise occupied. To his face when I told him I didn't want him. To his determination to respect my boundaries even though he doesn't understand them.

To how lonely he must feel with his dad being sick. My heart aches at the thought.

Without much control over my actions, I pull out my phone.

Laura: Are you okay?

I'm not sure what makes me ask it, but I need to know that he's not alone in his home thinking about how he doesn't have anyone to talk to. Which is ridiculous. I finally got exactly what I wanted—space from my soulmate so I can keep him safe. And now I'm undoing all that hard work.

Ugh, can I unsend that?

My phone buzzes. I take a beat to prepare for whatever he's going to say, to deep breathe. To meditate like Grandma taught me.

Fuck this.

Hulking Brute: Dad had a bad day today.

I hold the phone to my chest, trying to alleviate the ache. I don't even know Ash's dad, but I hate hearing that he had a bad day. I hate knowing Ash has to deal with this.

All I want is to find him and hug him.

How am I supposed to navigate this? How am I supposed to know what the right thing to do is?

I'm trying to protect him, I'm trying to give him the chance to find a life that isn't as dangerous as the one I unfortunately live. I'm trying to give him what he deserves.

Why does it seem like the more I get to know him, the more I don't know what I'm doing after all?

> Laura: Meet at our spot just before sunrise?

Good God, we have a spot.

> Hulking Brute: Thanks, Goldilocks. I'll see you then.

I just hope I don't regret it.

∼

WINTER MAY BE my favorite season. Lord knows why, though, considering it's fucking cold as a witch's tit out here.

But I can't deny the almost lonely beauty of a blanket of snow over a world undisturbed. The trees wait helplessly for the cold to fade away so they can bloom once more, while we all huddle inside in our warm blankets and body heat.

I pull up to the parking lot in my pink Prius—*not* the Pink Puke Mobile as Hazel calls it—to find Ash's behemoth of a truck already waiting. I'm not surprised, honestly, he seems the punctual type.

At my approach, he hops out of the car and my heart leaps similarly into my throat. He's beautiful, as usual, all wrapped up in layers of jackets that only highlight how broad he is.

But it isn't his beauty that captures my attention, it's his face. The sadness there. It's the sadness that pulls me out of my car and into his space.

We don't speak, but I can see the tension in his shoulders and the stress in the furrow of his brow. His smile in greeting is weak, it doesn't reach his eyes. Doesn't hold the same teasing lightness it usually does.

My body aches from the pain he's radiating. It's heartbreaking.

I follow him through the trees to our spot in the clearing with the view of the impending sunrise. It hasn't begun yet, but light tickles the tops of the trees.

I breathe deeply. "Is he okay?"

He nods, eyes trained ahead. "He's okay. Sometimes I swear the chemo makes him sicker than anything the cancer was doing to him."

"It must be hard watching him go through that."

A twinge of color dances above the tree line now. It won't be long until the sunrise.

"It's the worst thing I've ever been through." His voice trembles. "And there's not a goddamn thing I can do about it. I can't help him. The only thing that's helping him makes him sick as a dog and there's nothing I can do."

Every cell in my body screams at me to touch him. To hold his hand. To comfort him in some way.

Still, I hesitate.

"You're there for him. That's more than a lot of people do."

He chuckles, hollow and humorless. "He's my dad, of course I'm there for him."

"Not everyone feels that way about family. You're lucky you're so close." I finally give in, sliding my hand into his. Electric sparks skitter up my skin and down my spine. "Despite how much it hurts."

He squeezes my fingers, eyes dipping down to see the contact. As if he can't believe I actually touched him.

I can't believe I did either.

"Love is always worth the pain," he says softly, just as the sun breaks the tree line. His face is awash in pinks, reds, yellows, oranges, and blues. I'll remember his face in this moment for the rest of my fucking life.

The moment he gave the go-ahead.

The moment I dropped his hand.

I turn to the sunrise, trying to push down the swelling emotion. My eyes burn, but I refuse to close them. My heart beats so heavily, I swear it'll rip right out of my chest.

"It's freezing," I say, rubbing my hands together. "Should we head back?"

I'm probably giving him whiplash at this point.

He frowns, disappointment highlighting the lines beside his eyes.

The world hangs around us, practically stopping as he studies me. With one last nod, his shoulders sag. "All right, Goldilocks. Wouldn't want you freezing your dainty little legs off."

And just like that, we're back to our slightly antagonistic banter. I'm so much safer here, in my comfort zone. The softer side of him threatens to undo all my careful work.

CHAPTER 13
WHISPERS

Despite Grandma's disapproval, I bring the Pruitt family history book to the market with me. Most of my time is spent here waiting for people to buy something, so it's the perfect time to research.

Plus, I'm hoping if I look busy that Ash will stay away. I can't even bear to look at him after this morning. He's so good at pretending he doesn't have a care in the world, but there are soft, wounded places inside of him that deserve to be loved and cared for. By someone who won't kill him in the process.

Someone who isn't me.

The idea of him with someone else—kissing someone else, touching someone else, *fucking* someone else—causes jealousy thick and acidic to churn in my belly.

I think I'd hate every second of watching him move on with his life. Despite knowing it's what's best for him in the end.

My eyes flicker over the pages as I sift through the book. I feel like I've been through it five times, and I'm obviously missing something. I know I'm not the only Fire witch in existence, and I certainly can't be the only one in my family line.

That's ridiculous.

Wait.

There.

The word 'whispers' catches my eye. It's not 'fire,' but considering I'm barely paying attention to what I'm reading, it may be there anyway.

Virginia Pruitt, 1746. She would have been Elizabeth's great-granddaughter.

Let's see what you have for me, Virginia.

CHAPTER 14
VIRGINIA PRUITT

Virginia Pruitt was born in 1746, the daughter of Annabelle Pruitt Beckett and Timothy Beckett. She and her sister, Dorothy, were twins, raised together with knowledge of their magical background.

Just like the women before her, Virginia's powers manifested themselves when Virginia started her first course. It began with whispers, as she described them to her mother, from seemingly nowhere.

After months of testing elements, trying to see where Virginia's powers lay, they finally found the whispers coming from the candle flame.

Not much else is known about the early days of Virginia's training, as those journals were lost in a fire.

Virginia tragically went insane and died unexpectedly at the age of eighteen. Family historians have concluded it was a heart attack, but the nature of which is still unknown.

The family line continued through her twin sister, Dorothy.

CHAPTER 15

THAT'S NOT OMINOUS
AT ALL

That's not ominous at all.

Journals lost in a fire? Virginia dying of a heart attack at *eighteen*?

The math ain't mathing.

Something was up with her magic, and I have a feeling it was because she was a Fire witch. Maybe this is why we're the rarest type of elemental. Most of us don't make it that far in life.

I have to keep learning magic. I can't let Draven show up and fuck my family up even worse than he already has. No matter that I've had permanent goosebumps and a lump in my throat ever since I read the words 'heart attack.'

This is turning into a perfect fucking day. And it's going to get worse.

Because I have to talk to Hazel and Grandma about this. It's pretty clear I'm in over my head, and as stubborn as I'd like to be about it, I'm not trying to end up dead.

What even is my life at this point?

The flame on the scented candle next to me flickers and snaps, as if it's trying to get my attention.

"Don't you fucking start with me," I hiss at it. "I am very much not in the mood."

Now I'm fighting with fire. Awesome.

I need a shopping break. Shopping is second nature to me, if I'm shopping I don't have to think. I don't have to fixate on heart attacks and burned journals and the fact that Virginia was only eighteen.

With a nod, I stand. I place the 'back in fifteen minutes' sign on the table and stride off toward the accessories.

There's a yearning in my gaze as I look at all the bits and bobs, seeing part of the dreams I used to have. But I can't stay away from them. I can't help noticing the shifts in patterns, materials, and techniques.

I can't help wondering why I can't have my dreams.

THE BAGS I drag home from the market don't help me feel any better. I'm dreading this conversation, and no amount of shopping can change that.

Despite how desperately I tried.

My new purchases land with a *thunk* on my bed, rattling Belle, who decided to stay home today. She pointedly stares me down, then goes back to sleep.

Lazy princess.

The scent of dinner wafts up the stairs and into my room, an overwhelming amount of garlic. Not that I'll ever complain about there being too much garlic.

Here goes nothing.

The house creaks and groans in what I decide is solidarity as I quietly move through the home to the kitchen. Hazel's and Grandma's voices float through to the dining room. They're happy, talking about some details for Hazel's upcoming booth at the market. It's only a couple weeks until the new year and I haven't even gone Christmas shopping yet. I tried to find some things today, but I didn't find anything that I didn't overthink myself out of purchasing.

Fear of the impending conversation, of what is potentially happening to me, threatens to keep me standing here like a statue forever.

Belle is at my feet, nudging me forward. She seems much more aware than I give her credit for.

"Okay, okay, I'm going," I whisper-yell at her as she smushes her face into the backs of my knees.

She's at my side as I walk through the arch into the kitchen.

Hazel looks up, smile on her face. "Hey!"

"I—" I want to say it, but the words stick to the roof of my mouth like peanut butter. How do I tell them that I've barely learned anything, but what I have learned looks like an automatic death sentence?

Grandma turns at my tone, and now they're both staring at me.

"Here," I say instead, stuffing the book into Grandma's hands. "Virginia Pruitt."

Grandma reads quickly, Hazel mouthing along with the words over her shoulder. It's when Hazel's mouth stops moving and she's just standing there with her mouth hanging open that I get the distinct urge to run.

It's probably why Belle is standing directly behind me.

Traitor.

Grandma calmly closes the book, placing it beside her on the countertop. "I have known plenty of Fire witches in my day that have not died young. This ancestor lived over three hundred years ago and we have learned much since then. While I understand how scared you must be in this moment, I promise you're more worried than you should be."

"Plenty? How many is plenty?" My voice is slightly hysterical. Shrill and not as detachedly confident as I prefer.

She wraps me up in her arms and I soak in her scent. Lavender and smoke. "At least ten. We will figure out the whispering, and we'll do so in a way that keeps you safe."

I melt into the hug. I don't get enough hugs in a day.

Hazel wraps around me from behind and I'm in a Pruitt-witch sandwich. And I think I like it.

I'm becoming sentimental. Ew.

CHAPTER 16

WHAT ARE WE DOING?

Hulking Brute: You okay?

I stared at that text all night after talking to Hazel and Grandma. Even when I put my phone down to try and sleep, I saw it behind my closed eyelids. And then I dreamed of replying, of telling Ash I just wanted him to hold me.

To feel those giant arms around my waist, pulling me close so I can bury my face in his neck.

And now I've been staring at it all morning, while I sit at this stupid booth. Avoiding looking in his direction. The sounds of the market swirl around me but I can't hear them. The spicy winter scent tries to envelop me but I can't smell it.

Would it really be so horrible if I just gave in? Noah is still alive, so there's no guarantee that Ash would ever get hurt.

But on the other hand, both my mother and father are gone. And Noah did get kidnapped by a warlock, beaten, and put into a magical coma not too long ago.

I drop my head into my hands and groan. Before, I would just distract myself with sex. I could escape reality—escape being surrounded by a broken family—for just a little while. But I know in the very depths of my soul that having another man touch me would make me throw up.

Violently.

And I don't want random-man dick. I want big, thick, muscly, mountain-tree-man dick.

I want Ash. And isn't that terrifying? Am I going to be alone forever?

"Your phone broken?" Ash's voice makes me snap my head up so quickly, I'm momentarily concerned I have whiplash.

His eyes are a roiling storm. He's in the mood to fight and so am I.

Thank fuck.

"Nope! Why do you ask?" I snark, leaning back in the chair.

His fists clench, doing fantastic things to his biceps and fore-arms. "I sent you a text."

"Hmm." I glance at my phone. "Must've not seen it."

"You must've not—" A strangled laugh escapes him as he paces back and forth a couple times in front of me. "I was worried about you!"

"Not that worried if you only sent one text and didn't even try to call." I shoot him a smug smile. "Or are you one of those people who's afraid of talking on the phone? I promise, no one is gonna jump out and get you. You'll be okay."

His hands slam on the table, causing me to jump. In contrast, his eyes are full of pain and his voice is soft. "What are we doing, Goldilocks?"

No. No, no, no. I was enjoying the fighting, the fighting was good. Maybe not healthy, but good. Don't make me answer ques-tions I don't have the answers to.

"Having a little tiff over a text message?" I ask, trying to ignore the swelling panic in my chest. My cheeks flame as he stares at me.

His eyebrows draw together, the sternness in his face high-lighting the sharpness of his jaw. It's a jaw just screaming to be sat on.

"Am I supposed to know what's going on in your head?" he asks quietly, as if the words are forced out of him.

"I'm a riddle wrapped in a mystery wrapped in an enigma."

"And now you're quoting Churchill?" He exhales heavily. "I don't know what to do with you."

A bitter smile lifts the corners of my mouth. "Most people see me and think I'm stupid. Maybe it's the blonde hair, maybe it's the big boobs, but no one thinks I'm capable of knowing who Churchill is, let alone being able to quote him. You wouldn't be the first person not to know what to do with me."

It would suck if Ash underestimated me, too, but not surprising. No one looks at me and thinks 'intelligent woman.' At first, it was fun using my looks to surprise people. To catch them off guard. But I think as time has gone on, I've allowed people to see only that side of me. I've kept my mind to myself to keep myself safe.

"I've never said shit about you not being smart, so don't put words in my mouth. Ever since you first opened your gorgeous lips, I've known you could talk circles around me. What I'm trying to figure out is why the fuck you keep pushing me away. Every single time I think we're making progress, you switch it up and build those damn walls up again. I know what I want, Goldilocks, and that's you. I let you in. Why won't you do the same?"

My soulmate knows how to shut me up. I just wanted to fight, to twist every word he said into something I could poke at him for. And here he is, matching me beat for beat.

What do I say to that?

There's nothing I can say. So I don't. I just match his gaze and wait. Wait for him to realize that I won't answer this question. That I won't cross this line.

I've made a decision: I'm not letting myself have Ash Cedar and I won't go back on it.

He uses his hands on the table to push off, rocking back so he's standing straight. "Fine."

Then he's gone.
And he takes my heart with him.

CHAPTER 17

YOU SAID IT, NOT ME

The days weigh heavily on me, despite the good that is happening.

I'm finally getting a handle on my magic in a way that doesn't terrify me. Magic lessons have progressed to a point where I can summon fire easily and protect myself—minimally, but still. I don't feel as pathetically weak as I did when I watched my mother disappear in a swirling vortex of water. And the whispers have quietened to a manageable murmur that doesn't pull me under.

Hazel and I can be in the same room together without me wanting to cry or rip her hair out. We haven't had some of the heavier discussions that I know are ahead of us, but we can actually relate to each other again.

I feel useful, helping Grandma with selling her wares at the market. And I'm thoroughly enjoying spending time around other witches, hearing the gossip and immersing myself in the community.

All of that, and all I can think about is Ash. About how we're in this strange stalemate, about how I refuse to take those steps forward.

Watching Noah and Hazel doesn't help. I don't understand half of what they say to each other—nerd language is not my forte—but the love is overwhelming. I honestly think he may propose soon, despite them not being together long. Or at least ask her to move in with him.

She just moved back into the house, but I think it would be good for her to be with him. It's obvious that it's what they both want.

I wonder if she's letting the guilt she feels in relation to me keep her from him.

I'm not the only one watching them, either. Grandma has tears in her eyes a lot more than she used to, especially when she looks at them. She wants a soulmate, but she never found hers.

How angry would she be with me if she knew I'd found mine and I'm refusing to be with him?

It baffles me that I'm the only one of us who is trying to keep their soulmate safe. To protect them. A niggling part of my brain tries to point out that I'm really trying to protect *myself*, but that part sounds like a bitch, so I don't listen.

What does she know anyway?

I don't want to spend the rest of my life alone, but isn't choosing to spend it alone better than being forced to?

"Where is your head, Laura dear?" Grandma asks, pulling my attention to her. Hazel and Noah are off on some special date, so Grandma asked me to have a private magical lesson with her in the garden. She hasn't pushed me to go back to the magic shop, and for that I'm eternally grateful.

Even if it means sitting on cold ground.

I smile sadly. "Sorry, Grandma."

"You know you can talk to me." She places her hand on mine. We're sitting opposite each other outside on our customary pillows. The bangles on her wrist jangle with every motion.

Could I really talk to her about this? Would Grandma be angry like I imagine, or would she understand?

"I have something fairly personal on my mind . . ." I trail off.

She nods. "No judgment. I promise."

"If you could find your soulmate, knowing what we know and watching people we love die like we have, would you do it?"

Her eyes flick over to the garden she still maintains for Mom. Her brows furrow as she contemplates my question.

I appreciate that she doesn't just answer off the cuff, that she considers what I'm asking and gives it true thought.

"Yes, I would. None of us are guaranteed anything in this life, but love is always worth it," she says, turning back to me. "Any of us could die at any moment, not from anything magical or daemonic, but that's certainly no reason not to enjoy the beautiful things that life has to offer. Love included."

My eyes burn. I knew she'd say something like that, but I didn't want her to. I wanted her to agree with me.

"A certain someone at the market?" she asks softly.

I blush under her scrutinizing gaze. She knows exactly who I'm talking about, but I wouldn't say his name even if I were being waterboarded.

"And you don't want to move forward because you're scared he'll get hurt? Because of what happened with your father and Noah?"

I nod. "And Mom."

Tears shine in her eyes. "I think that's entirely understandable. And no one is going to convince you otherwise until you're ready."

That's oddly validating. My thought process isn't so ridiculous that Grandma can't follow the logic. "But you think I'm wrong?"

"I'm not going to tell you what you feel is wrong. That would be unfair and incorrect. You feel the way you feel. But I think working through those feelings may lead you to a different perspective."

I laugh. "Way to say I'm wrong without saying it."

She shrugs, a soft smile dancing on her lips. "You said it, not me."

We chuckle together, the heaviness of the conversation lifting off our shoulders and into the cold winter evening.

I don't know what I'm going to do, but I do know I'm not going to do anything until I'm ready. And not a minute before.

CHAPTER 18

SAY IT

The next day at the market, Hazel shows up as the day is winding down to drop off some merchandise.

"Why do you keep looking at me?" I finally demand after thirty minutes of her flicking her eyes over to me like I'm some sort of fancy museum exhibit.

Her smile is conspiratorial, as if we were just gabbing about a secret. "I . . . Well, I got home early last night, and I may have accidentally overheard part of your conversation with Grandma."

Fucking shit.

"Leave it alone," I demand.

Drop it, Hazel. Please drop it.

"Is he really? Is Ash really . . ." She trails off.

She's not going to drop it.

I huff a frustrated breath. "What? Is he *what*?"

All the good feelings from my conversation with Grandma fall away, leaving the twisted anger and fear that burn like flame in my gut. I'm not ready to share this with her. I purposely *didn't* share this with her, and crossing my boundaries like this is bullshit.

"Is he your soulmate?"

I cringe at the word. I'm not a liar, but I know what she'll say.

She'll tell me that I deserve love, that I deserve what she and Noah have. It'll be meant as a compliment, but it isn't one. Do I deserve to lose the one I love? To turn into a monster because I got the person I love kidnapped or killed?

I like to think I don't deserve that.

The scent of warm fire, evergreen trees, and musk overwhelms me. Fuck.

"Answer her."

I turn to find Ash standing there, radiating palpable frustration. His normally evergreen eyes are a forest in the middle of a storm.

I can't force air from my lungs—no words or breath. I'm consumed by the myriad of emotions pouring off him. The cautious optimism that flutters around him like fireflies at dusk. The frustration of being held at arm's length. The longing that clenches his fists.

"Answer her, Goldilocks," he repeats, his voice trembling just a tad.

Shit.

I open and close my mouth a few times. My silence is more powerful than anything I could've said.

Hazel's mouth falls open as she watches the exchange, as she watches Ash take one single step forward.

"Hazel, I need a moment with her." Ash turns to my sister. "Please."

"Are you okay with that?" she asks me quietly.

Now she's considerate of my feelings. Now, when she's already done a world of damage.

I nod.

Despite not wanting to face this conversation, despite being forced before I was ready, I know I'm safe with Ash.

She leaves, closing the flap of the tent behind her to give us some semblance of privacy. But I know those old biddies now. We'll be the topic of gossip for days.

"I knew there was something different between us." His body

trembles. "I knew what we have is more than anything I've ever felt in my life. The way I'm drawn to you, the way I've memorized the cadence of your voice. My entire being is yours and I've barely touched you."

I take a small step backward. I'm not ready for this.

I can't.

"Do you know how often I think about touching you? Goldilocks, I swear to fuck I am a man possessed by the idea of simply holding your hand. And here you are, knowing exactly what we are to each other. I suspected, sure, but with how hard you pushed me away I was half-convinced I was insane. Were you ever going to tell me?"

I take another small step back.

"Say something!" he begs, hope and desperation dripping from every word. "Anything!"

"You're my soulmate," I whisper into the tent. I admit the one thing I've been trying to avoid since the moment he first touched me. Because it doesn't change anything.

It doesn't matter.

His hand covers his heart, rubbing at his thick flannel as if he could soothe the ache on his own. "I knew it."

We stare at each other. Absorb the heaviness, the weight of us.

"How long have you known?" he asks.

I'm not surprised he has questions. I just really don't want to fucking answer them. I don't want to keep hurting him. I just wanted to stay away.

But no! Grandma had to force me to open this stupid booth, and he had to keep coming around after I kept trying to set boundaries.

"Since the first time you touched me. Since fall."

"For months?" Betrayal flashes in his eyes. He takes a cautious step forward. Just one, but it feels like so much more. "You've known for months, and you . . . You really were never going to tell me. You were going to keep going on with your life and never say a goddamn word. Why?"

Anger swoops up into my throat. "Because it's what I decided to do. I'm an adult and I made a decision about my life. I don't answer to you!"

"No." He advances again as if he needs to be close to me. Needs the reassurance of my presence and warmth just as much as I need his. But he's still a few feet away. "You sure as hell don't answer to me, Goldilocks, but you made a decision about *our* lives. You don't get to make decisions that include me without even the courtesy of a discussion."

"Do you feel so much better now?" I step forward, closing the distance one extra foot, scrabbling for control over this conversation. "Do you feel better knowing that you're my soulmate and I didn't tell you? That I didn't want to tell you? Is it better than me suffering in fucking silence? Is both of us suffering with the weight of this really that much better?"

His chuckle is low and full of pain. "As if I wasn't already suffering. At least now I know why."

I blink back the stinging in my eyes. The pain in my chest begs me to run to him. To let him hold me and take care of me. To soothe away this awfulness.

He's there, wiping away the first tear before it can even fall. Electricity pulses from his skin through mine, wrenching a gasp from both of us.

"You don't get to make decisions for me anymore. Going forward, we make decisions together," he says.

I shake my head. I know I'm right. Aren't I?

I won't turn into my mom. And what if it was the opposite? What would it do to him if I were the one he lost?

"I am so fucking pissed at you," he growls, leaning his forehead against mine. "For trying to take this from us. For doing it without thinking I deserved to know. I've never been angrier."

Everything I've been trying to avoid—all the pain I tried to keep from him—is right there on his face. All my plans and hopes are dissolved in the blink of an eye.

"I'm not sorry for trying to protect you from this," I whisper.

"And I'm not sorry either."

Before I can ask for what, his hand comes up to cradle my cheek. The soft action contrasts with the rough calluses on his hand from all the woodwork. With one last breath, his lips press to mine.

And the world melts away.

His full lips are gentle, but the anger is there simmering under the surface. A grunt is my only warning before my back is pressed against the wood beam holding the tent up.

I dig my fingers into his shoulders, needing him closer. The hand on my cheek slips down to my neck, thumb rubbing against my pulse point.

My mind is liquid. All I know is his body, his touch, the electric current running between our bodies, making everything that much more sensitive. I think I'd come apart if he touched me anywhere else.

My mouth opens at his nip to my lower lip, and he delves inside.

Why did I ever *not* want this?

"See, Goldilocks?" His mouth moves down my neck, nibbling and sucking. "You feel that? You fucking belong to me, and I never want to hear you say anything otherwise."

I am a woman possessed. I hike my leg up to his waist and he grabs it, grinding me into the harsh wooden pole at my back.

"Say it, Goldilocks. Say you belong to me and I'll show you exactly what you've been missing." He bites my neck.

Words? My body rolls against his, feeling every inch of his hard, muscular body. What I wouldn't give to feel the power he must have.

"Say it, and I'll kneel before you. I'll worship you in the middle of this tent for the entire fucking market to hear. I'll let you ride my tongue until you cum so hard it tears this world in half."

I moan at the way my nipples harden, brushing against his chest. Too much. It's too much.

He pulls away just a fraction, keeping my leg up in his hand. His smile is triumphant. "Say it."

"I'm yours."

I'm yours.

The words fly out of my mouth at his demand and there's no way to take them back.

Ash's hand caresses my thigh, mapping out every part of me he can. "Let me taste you. Please."

I take his face in my hands, forcing his lips back to mine. I want to enjoy the blissful emptiness of my mind before the doubts come back.

His beard scratches against my skin in the most delightful burn, his touch like a brand. I'll never be the same.

"You've driven me mad," he whispers in my ear, sucking on the lobe. "You've driven me half-mad."

You have no idea what madness is.

Madness is touching the one person in this world you want more than anything and still fearing every second of it. Of having your soulmate in your arms and trembling with terror.

"Shut up," I snap, digging my fingers into his hair. "No more words, for fuck's sake."

His mouth is harsh as he nips and sucks at my neck, bruising my skin. I'll have marks for days and I can't bring myself to regret the possessiveness in each one.

Fingers play with the button of my jeans, digging in just a bit to tease the sensitive skin there. His eyes meet mine, not needing to voice the question behind them.

My breaths come in heavy pants, but my mind has cleared enough that panic has seeped in. I don't break our connection, liquid-emerald pools watching me as if I'm both the bane of his existence and his redemption.

"I have . . ." I swallow, my mouth suddenly dry as desert sand. "I have dinner with my family. I have to go."

Annoyance flickers across his eyes before he takes a deep breath. "We have to talk about this."

"We will. We will, I just have to go. I have to."

My heart speeds up as anxiety threatens to swallow me. I can't be here.

"There's no air in here!" I exclaim, breaking out of his hold. I run to the tent flap and throw it open, taking in deep breaths of the outside world.

He stands there, his arms still up in the same position, as if my reaction has surprised him so much he can't move. It probably has.

I'm fully aware I'm acting absolutely illogically. I'm erratic and panic-ridden and I have to get out of here.

I can't stand the way he's staring at me, the way I've done exactly what I promised myself I wouldn't.

And the way most of me doesn't regret it. Most of me wants to run back to his arms.

"Laura," he says, all the pain and misery in the world in one single word. In the name he never uses.

My knees wobble as I stare out at the market, not truly seeing anything. I can't imagine what I must look like to everyone.

"Please," I say, turning to him. "Please, Ash."

"After dinner? After dinner with your family can we talk?"

I should say no. But I crossed the line today, and he deserves some sort of explanation as to why this can't continue. Why I have to be stronger now, despite knowing it'll be that much harder.

I nod. "I'll text you."

"Will you really?"

The doubt is fair, but it hurts nonetheless.

"Yes, I promise. I don't go back on promises."

My skin aches in each spot he touched me as we simply watch each other from opposite sides of the tent. I wish his soulmate could've been someone safer for him.

"I'll find you even if you do."

Despite everything, the corner of my mouth lifts in a half smile. "I know you will."

From the way that man looks at me, I know he would follow me into the depths of Hell and back. And that's what terrifies me.

CHAPTER 19
SHOT TO KILL

"What in the *actual fuck*, Hazel?" I scream the moment I get home. The house goes silent for a moment as the door slams shut behind me. I can't believe she opened her big, fat mouth and spilled the soulmate beans.

All through the drive home, anger toward my sister built and built—and now I swear I'm like a volcano about to erupt. Hot lava roils in my belly.

She ruined everything. She took away my life, she changed everything, and now she's torn down all my carefully crafted plans to keep Ash away from all this bullshit. Without a single care in the world!

The rational part of my brain understands she didn't really have anything to do with my life changing so much. That everything with Draven was going to hit us whether she left the house or not. But anger isn't rational, and definitely not today.

Nothing about me is logical today.

She's cringing as she rounds the corner from the kitchen. "I am so sorry, Laura. I had no idea he was right there, and definitely no idea you didn't want him to know."

Noah comes up behind her as she speaks, rubbing her back.

"Considering I never mentioned it to you, that doesn't really matter. It was none of your fucking business!"

"I just got excited." She holds her hands up in surrender. "I was excited for you to have a soulmate. To have someone, and for me to have someone to talk about this with."

"Oh, you're excited for me? You're excited that I now have someone who will be in harm's way constantly? That I will have to deal with the fear of losing someone else? That I have someone who can be used against me, to hurt me?" It's spewing out of me like fire, and I can't control it. I'm just so fucking mad.

"I had no idea you felt that way." Her face falls. "I'm sorry."

"Stop repeating that you're sorry! It doesn't change anything. It doesn't change that you have once again trampled through my life without any regard for the damage you do."

Noah steps forward. "Maybe we should all take a breath, make sure we aren't saying things out of anger that we'll regret later."

Hazel sighs, putting her hand on Noah's shoulder. "I got this."

"Do you? Because you seem to just bulldoze around like a bull in a china shop with no regard for anyone but yourself!" My entire body vibrates as I stare them down. I want them to be scared, I want them to do something to change the fact that everything in my life is different.

"All I have ever done is try to protect you, to give you everything you ever needed. And the one time I did something for me, you had a hissy fit!" Hazel says, wind whipping around her hair.

Good. Fight me, bitch.

"As if being my surrogate parent didn't stroke your martyr kink. Don't act like you didn't get something out of being the victim your entire life. That is, until you decided you were too good for me and abandoned me like a sack of kittens on the side of the road."

"Screw you, Laura," she whispers.

"Even now you're doing it," I say, unable to stop poking at her.

"I bet you said it in front of Ash on purpose just to further punish me for being such a burden to you for so many years."

One tear falls down Hazel's cheek; she rears back as if she's been slapped. She went low, but I went lower.

She aimed to wound, but I shot to kill.

I step back, guilt gnawing at me. The anger still licks at my skin, but the haze clears a little at her tear.

I've gone too far tonight. In trying to avoid thinking about Ash, I've let myself get twisted up in anger and explode.

"I'll stay somewhere else tonight. Make sure Belle is fed," I mumble, and turn to leave. The guilt weighs on every creaking step I take toward the door. The house isn't happy with my outburst, or with my leaving.

But the house can deal with it.

The tears don't fall until I'm in my car.

CHAPTER 20
CRUEL ENOUGH

I'm not in the car for more than three minutes before my phone rings. I look down at the screen. Ash Cedar.

Stupid soulmate bond.

I click the button on my steering wheel to answer. "Yeah?"

"What's going on?" Ash's concerned voice fills the car.

I huff a pained laugh, tears spilling onto my lap. "Just got into it with sister dearest. I'm fine."

I'm the furthest damn thing from fine.

"Do you want me to come to you?"

I haven't moved from the driveway, but I said I'd leave for the night and no part of me wants to go back inside. Especially not with Ash in tow.

"I'll come to you. Text me your address."

The last thing I want to do tonight is get into it with him. I don't think I have the emotional capacity to think right now, let alone have this sort of conversation. But I promised I'd talk to him.

And I don't go back on promises.

"All right, Goldilocks. I'll have some drinks ready."

"Thank fuck for that."

The drive is easy. Driving is relaxing, mechanical, routine in a way that allows me to turn my brain off. I once said that to Hazel and she chewed my ear off for an hour about how I needed to always be aware while driving.

The thought of her brings a fresh wave of pain, slicing through my chest. I went too fucking far tonight. But it was like word-vomit. Once I started, I just couldn't stop.

It's probably proof that I'm holding way too much shit in. Instead of addressing my feelings about her leaving, about our distance, I let it build up inside me until something small set me off.

At least she has Noah with her. I'm glad she has someone to comfort her, even if I'm the reason she needs comforting.

I turn on to a secluded drive and am immediately submerged in darkness. It's a private lane in the middle of nowhere, but that fits Ash. He wouldn't live in some high-rise or cookie-cutter neighborhood.

He belongs in the woods.

Headlights illuminate the log cabin and it almost startles a laugh out of me. I said he belongs in the woods, but a log cabin is a little on the nose. A giant tree trunk sits to the side with an axe sticking out of it.

Because of course he splits his own wood. No wonder his shoulders are so massive.

And then he's there, standing in the doorway. He's in a long-sleeved green Henley, rolled up to his elbows, that matches his eyes and gray sweatpants.

That's goddamn unfair. He must know that's an outfit right out of a romance novel. And all I want is to lose myself in the fantasy.

I step out of the car, watching as he leans against his door-frame, arms crossed. Even just being in his presence is a balm on my frayed nerves.

I understand why Hazel wanted Noah close when she and I

were fighting. All I feel right now is a physical pull toward Ash. He's grounding, safe, in a way that I've never experienced. Calm in a storm.

How much of that is the soulmate bond, and how much is just Ash? I don't know if I'll ever be able to separate the two ideas enough to find out.

"Come here, stubborn woman," he growls, the words rumbling out of his chest and across the driveway—if you could call it that. It's really just a gravel trail worn by years of tire marks.

For once, I don't fight him. In a moment I'm in his arms, burying my head in his chest. Warm fires, evergreen trees, and musk. My safe place.

If my willingness to do what he asks surprises him, he doesn't let on. Just wraps his arms around me and pulls me closer.

I melt into him and the buzzy comfort of our electricity.

"Tonight's not the night for all we have to talk about. Come inside anyway," he whispers into my hair, the low tones of his voice speaking to the scared woman inside me. To the little girl who never felt seen. To the young woman who forces it.

I nod, wordlessly thanking him for letting me off the hook. For knowing exactly what it is I need without having to voice it. My hands crawl up his chest and around the back of his neck, playing with the tiny little hairs at the base.

He draws me inside, keeping us connected and closing the door behind us. I refuse to lift my head from his chest as he maneuvers us through his home, but he doesn't complain.

He plops on the couch, pulling me on top of him.

I lift my eyes and find myself face-to-face with him, knees straddling his thighs and closer than we've ever been.

"Hi," I say softly into the inch of space between us.

He really is a beautiful man. Devastatingly so.

"Hey, Goldilocks. How are you?"

I shrug, little lightning shocks going up and down my back in rhythm with his fingertips. "Rough day."

His nose nuzzles against mine. "Mm. What can I do for you?"

I have an entire damn list of things he could do for me. To me. It's not fair to go there without talking about it, and I don't want to be cruel.

I've been cruel enough today.

"Can we drink and not talk about anything serious? And then fall asleep?" I ask, digging my fingers into his shoulders.

His mouth lifts in a smile. "Yeah, we can do that."

"WE'RE GOING to take turns guessing something about the other person, and if you're wrong then you drink. If you're right, the other person drinks," I explain as Ash hands me a glass of wine. I frown at it. "Nothing stronger?"

"Trust me, you'll be wrong enough that you'll still get drunk," he quips, sitting on the other end of the couch from me with his beer.

I huff. "Yeah, but wine-drunk is different. Wine-drunk is sad and headachey and hangover city. Don't you have vodka or tequila or something?"

"You really think tequila is going to give you a better hangover tomorrow?"

"No, but I'll be so drunk I won't care."

"Luckily for you, I don't have tequila. Your choices are whisky, beer, and wine."

"I'm surprised it's not moonshine."

"Make your first guess, Goldilocks," he says instead of continuing the banter. Rude.

Hmm. What do I think I know about this man?

"I'm guessing the last musical artist you listened to wears a lot of flannel."

"You're right, actually. It was Hozier. Specifically the song 'Sunlight.'" He tips the beer bottle back, exposing the long line of his neck as he drinks. Who knew necks could be sexy?

I clear my throat. "Surprisingly good taste. What draws you to him?"

The moment his eyes darken, I regret asking. "The man knows about worshiping a woman. He doesn't sing about cutesy crushes, he sings about all-encompassing love. The kind of love you drown in. The kind of love that burns you alive."

I'm speechless. The urge to crawl back into his lap is almost too much, but somehow I resist.

"I guess that your favorite color is dark red. Blood red," he says, his voice lowered and soft. Enticing.

"Not pink?"

"Not pink. You *like* pink, don't get me wrong, and you don't mind letting other people think it's pink. But even if it's not red, it's not pink."

Without answering verbally, I sip the wine. It's sweet, but not ridiculously so. Dark chocolatey and warm in a way that fits this warm home. This warm environment he's created.

He relaxes back into the corner of the off-white couch with a cocky smile. He's entirely too proud of himself and it makes me want to beat him.

I play with the rim of my glass. "I guess that you love all animals but are more of a dog person."

He tips his head. "We already talked about this, Goldilocks."

"I didn't agree not to cheat."

He smiles. "I do prefer dogs, but don't tell Belle."

His beer is half-gone already.

I squirm under the pressure of the tension between us. It's as thick as smog. Heat licks at the base of my spine and I drop my eyes to my half-full glass.

I can't give in yet.

"I guess you're smarter than everyone gives you credit for," he says. I snap my head up to meet his gaze. "I guess that you've spent your entire life being underestimated as the pretty one, when really you don't fit into any of those neat little boxes people like to put others in. You are stunningly beautiful, but you're also quick witted and intelligent. Competitive. Caring, when you want to be. Stubborn, too."

My mouth is dry. "How am I supposed to answer that?"

"You're supposed to drink, Goldilocks. Those are the rules, aren't they?"

"Only if you guessed right."

"Exactly. Drink."

The dominance in his tone should absolutely not cause a burn low in my belly, but I take a deep drink of wine anyway, licking the droplets from my lips.

His hand comes up, rubbing the tip of his thumb against my mouth. I lean into it for a moment—two—and pull back.

I've set a boundary for tonight, and I'm determined not to cross it.

"I—" my voice comes out shaky, uncertain. "I guess you own at least ten pairs of jeans."

He snorts, scratching his chin. "Would you like to go count?"

"In your bedroom?"

His eyebrow cocks in a teasing way. "That's where the closet is."

That feels like a danger zone. "You don't know how many pairs of jeans you own?"

"I haven't counted lately, no. But I'd be willing to drink if you don't want to go in there."

I nod, and he polishes off his beer.

He stands. "More wine?"

I nod again, no words able to escape me as he crosses into the kitchen. At least, I assume it's the kitchen. The room is walled off and hidden behind a wooden door.

I bet it's a small kitchen. Something warm and homey, perfect for dinners with his dad and a few friends.

It's all very *Little House on the Prairie* meets Lumberjack-core.

The desire to explore without him hovering over me is strong, but I stay glued to the couch regardless. I'm hyper-aware of every action I take and it's making me anxious.

"My turn, right?" he asks as he steps into the room. Wine and beer in hand.

I sigh. "Yes."

"Don't sound so excited. It was your idea to play this game." He tops off my wine glass before setting the bottle on the coffee table.

"Patiently waiting, brute," I reply. The nickname doesn't fit him anymore. If I'm honest, it never did. It was just a pathetic attempt to keep him at arm's length.

He smiles, an honest and pure thing that tugs at my own lips. "I guess you are an absolute horror to play boardgames with."

"There may have been a few incidents that caused my old friends to decide to not play with me." I drink. "But I'll have you know, they were just being sore losers."

"Of course they were," he laughs. "I'd play with you any day."

Oh, I didn't need the image of us playing together in my head. All the delightful, sinful things we could do together if I would just *let* him.

"Where did your head go?" he murmurs, scooting toward me.

"None of your business," I reply. My voice is soft, breathy, and I don't think I like this game anymore. I don't like knowing just how carefully he's been watching me, learning me. Knowing me.

He pays attention to me like no one ever has.

"Unfortunately for you, everything about you is my business. You're allowed your secrets, your feelings, all the things you want to keep private. But you are my business."

"You've made that pretty clear, considering how well you apparently know me."

His eyes trail from my legs up to my chest and face. It's thorough, but not lewd. Appreciative, but not vulgar. "Knowing you is a privilege I plan on earning."

"Could we—" I swallow around a dry throat. "Could we watch a movie?"

And save me from having to endure the intimacy of this discussion?

He shakes his head, fondness evident in the easy way he smiles. "Go ahead and pick something off Streemz, Goldilocks. I'll grab some popcorn."

"Extra butter and salt?"

"Wouldn't dream of anything else."

CHAPTER 21

DOOMED

I'm going to combust.

I could do it—my ancestors apparently did. It wouldn't be that difficult, and it especially wouldn't be difficult now.

I stare at the sprawling, custom-size bed dominating Ash's lumberjack-wet-dream bedroom and want to burst into actual flame. The movie is over, and if I thought two hours of low lights and moments of skin brushing against skin would be easier than that game . . . Well, let's just say I was completely wrong.

"This is my room," Ash says softly from behind me. Entirely unnecessarily, really.

"Of course it is, what else would it be?" I snap back, no real bite in my tone.

He only chuckles in reply to my attitude. "Would you like to borrow something to sleep in, or did you bring some PJs in that teeny tiny purse of yours?"

"Your arrogance is astounding." I run a hand through my blonde waves. "Obviously I'll have to borrow something, but I don't know how I'll fit. You're—what—eight feet tall and seven hundred pounds?"

"Six foot seven, and you never ask a person's weight." He gives me a mock glare. "It's rude."

"No wonder I feel like a pixie next to you! You're an actual forest creature!"

"And you like it. I'll grab you a t-shirt."

I refuse to verbally agree with him, because it's quite obvious I like it. He's huge and while I'm not almost miniature-sized like Hazel, he makes me feel small. Protected.

How entirely patriarchy coded.

I take another step forward into his space. This bed may be large, but no space is large enough when it comes to me and Ash. How am I supposed to share a bed with him?

He emerges from the closet with a shirt in hand, but that's not the part that steals the very breath from my lungs.

His own shirt is gone.

The man is built like a god. Muscles on muscles on muscles, poured into a delicious vee pointing straight to a bulge that I don't think anything could hide. Gray sweatpants are both the best and worst invention ever created.

He has black hair on his chest following the musculature, and it somehow heightens how perfectly crafted he is.

"You're staring," he says, leaning against the doorframe of the walk-in closet.

"You're half-naked," I reply, my voice breathier than I'd have liked.

He shrugs in agreement. "Fair point. You should probably join me."

My heart leaps, galloping like wild horses in the summer sun. Trying to run to him, no doubt.

"Ash . . ." I don't know how to finish the statement. I just keep hurting and hurting him. Hurting Hazel. Hurting everyone. All I want is to be left alone and safe, and to not hurt anybody anymore.

Understanding softens his face as he approaches me. His palm slides along my cheek, his comforting electric buzz soothing my nerves. "I wouldn't ever push you. We can just sleep."

I close my eyes, reveling in his touch despite knowing I shouldn't. The way his calluses brush against my skin.

"You really are the most beautiful woman I've ever seen. I knew the moment I first saw you I'd seen a goddess walking among men."

"The first moment I saw you, I knew I was doomed," I reply, opening my eyes. "I knew my life would never be the same."

His fist clenches in my hair, tilting my head up toward his. "Then stop fighting us."

"No."

Frustration rips a growl from his chest, rumbling against me. He slides his nose against mine. "Let me take care of you, Goldilocks. Let me show you that you don't need to fight this entire world alone. Let me give you everything you deserve. Let me give you everything."

I lift my hands to his chest, the softness of his skin contrasting the hardness of the muscle beneath.

"Let me," he repeats.

I squeeze my eyes shut against the intimacy of his gaze. I can't give in. I can't.

"My darling," he whispers. His other hand wraps around my waist, pulling us flush together. "Let me."

I melt into his touch, but don't say yes. I know he won't push me, won't kiss me, until I say yes to what he needs.

"And if I run away in the morning?"

"I won't allow it." He kisses my forehead. "As determined as you are to keep me away, you can't."

"I can," I reply. My voice is shaky. He's winning and he knows it.

"No, Goldilocks. You're mine, and there's no walking that back. Say it and let me kiss you."

My lashes flutter against the urge to open them, to meet what I know is a piercing emerald gaze full of love and stubbornness.

"I'm yours," I reply. "Kiss me."

He doesn't kiss me immediately, despite finally getting my okay.

He waits.

Waits until I finally open my eyes and face his liquid-forest stare. Waits for me to see the joy, the pure, unfiltered joy. Then slowly dips down to take my mouth.

He's slow, soft. Our first kiss was angry, frustration-fueled passion based on weeks—months—of buildup.

But this?

This is all the soft feelings underneath, the ones that threaten to burn down all the carefully constructed walls I've spent so long building. An adoration that I've spent my life craving and pushing away.

My fingers dig into the muscles of his chest as I tip my head back to allow him better access. He practically leaps at the opportunity, sucking my lip into his mouth and nibbling on the sensitive, kiss-swollen flesh.

"Will you let me touch you?" he asks, hand tightening in my hair in a way that's just on the right side of pleasurable.

As if I'm capable of saying anything but yes at this point. Fighting him takes so much energy, so much effort, and I can't pretend right now. I'm exhausted and I just want him to make me feel something other than alone, scared, and angry for the first time in weeks.

"Please," I whisper.

"While I enjoy hearing you beg," he says, hand on my waist traveling lower until he squeezes my ass. "You never have to beg for me, Goldilocks. I'll give you everything I have the power to give, you just have to tell me what you want."

"I want to forget about life. To turn off my brain. To relax and feel cared for. I . . ." My eyes plead for him to understand.

He shushes me, face full of kindness. "I've got you. You're safe with me. Relax."

"I'm going to be such a pillow princess."

He bends for a second, lifting me by the thighs into his arms. "That a fucking promise?"

I lean in close, my lips just barely brushing against his. "It can be."

He tosses me so I fall back on the bed with a whoosh of breath. I scoot up toward the pillows as he stands there, chest heaving at the end of the bed.

Throw me around, daddy.

"Do you know how many times I've imagined you like this? On my bed?" One knee falls to the bed as he crawls over my body until he's hovering above me. "Do you know how often I've imagined what you'll smell like? Taste like? Sound like?"

I practically pout. "Then why are you dragging it out?"

He shakes his head. "Savoring. I'm savoring every second."

His hands find the base of my shirt and drag it up, slowly exposing each new inch of skin. When my lacy, red bralette is revealed, he groans.

"Like it?"

"You're trying to kill me," he replies, palming the side of my ribs. His thumbs just barely grazing underneath the lace.

"I like pretty things," I counter. "And the look on your face is worth it."

My shirt hits the floor with a gentle hiss of fabric. His fingers pluck at the button on my jeans before he pulls them down my legs to join the shirt.

"Give me your mouth," he demands, all patience apparently gone. His lips are harsh, demanding, and only serve to wind my body up to a fever pitch.

His hands are everywhere. Pressing, smoothing, discovering every single inch of my body as if he may never get another chance.

That doubt is understandable.

"Beautiful," he murmurs, mouth pressing to the center of my chest. "Exquisite."

Before I can reply, he drags down the fabric of my bralette with his teeth, sucks a nipple into his mouth, and my back bows. The wetness and the electricity meld together into an almost-but-not-quite over-stimulating sensation that has me suddenly on the brink already.

"So responsive." Pride drips from his voice as his teeth nip just a little. "So desperate for my touch. My mouth."

"How'd I know you wouldn't shut up in bed?" I pant, practically overwhelmed with need for him to do *something* more. Anything.

He chuckles, whipping the bralette over my head. "You are the most stunning creature I've ever seen."

"Obviously."

"Confident. Sexy. A woman who knows her worth."

"Oh my God, will you stop talking and just touch me already?" I demand.

"I am touching you." His smile is downright devious. "Tell me what you want, and you can have it."

"If you're going to make me do everything, then I can just go home to my vibrator and do it myself."

He captures my nipple between thumb and forefinger, teasing the taut bud. "Next time, I'll tie you down and use your vibrator to make you cum until you sob."

Wetness pools between my thighs so quickly little goose-bumps prickle all over my skin. "Promises, promises."

He trails kisses down my body, nibbling just a moment on my belly button before meeting the top of my red lace underwear. He pulls them off slowly, dragging lingering kisses down my legs until my mind is a warm puddle. Until all I can think about is the next touch, the next kiss, the pleasure building.

"You smell so goddamn good. Every time I'm around you, I smell melted marshmallows and brown sugar. I can't wait to see if you taste the same."

Before I can form some sort of reply, his mouth is on me. He's no longer gentle and slow. No.

His tongue dives for my clit, sucking it into his mouth and flicking at it so quickly I can barely breathe.

His groan of pleasure vibrates through my body like an electric shock.

"Tastes like fucking heaven," he growls. A finger enters my body, curling just right to hit that spot inside of me that wrenches a gasp from the depths of my soul.

"Cum for me. Take what you need and give this to me."

Despite it only being a few minutes—seconds, maybe—I can feel an orgasm creeping up. The way my body responds to him is otherworldly.

"Laura," he growls. "Laura, my goddess."

My name is what tips me over, what causes waves of white-hot pleasure to roll through my body until I'm an overstimulated mess.

He slowly withdraws, biting my thighs just roughly enough to leave marks for a few hours.

"Tell me when you're ready for more."

CHAPTER 22

HOME

It takes what feels like years for my mind to clear the smoky fog of orgasm. I've never experienced something that powerful before.

Or that quick. I don't think I lasted more than a fucking minute.

My hands unclench from the bedspread below me and slide onto his chest and into his hair. His semi-short dark hair that's softer than angel wings.

Orgasms make me mushy.

He makes me mushy.

Ash is triumphant. His eyes glitter like melted forests and pride emanates from his skin.

"Do you need to go wipe your face?" I ask, finally getting my voice back. I won't be surprised if I'm hoarse for a few days if the night continues like this.

His beard is almost dripping with the evidence of how much he made me feel. "Why the fuck would I ever do that? I earned this."

"Whatever floats your boat, bruh."

"Do not call me 'bruh' in bed, woman." He narrows his eyes. "Matter of fact, don't ever call me 'bruh.'"

I stretch languorously, enjoying the way his eyes trail along my skin, unable to choose where to look. "Whatever should I call you then?"

"Ash." He presses a kiss to my belly button. "Sweetheart." A kiss to the center of my chest. "Boyfriend." A kiss to my collarbone. "Soulmate." A kiss to my lips. So quick I barely have time to respond.

"I don't—" I swallow the lump of emotion threatening to break through. "I don't remember agreeing to all that."

His smile is soft, understanding. "I'm yours, Goldilocks, and you're mine. Even if you run your perfectly toned ass out of here in the morning and deny us all over again. You and me? We're inevitable. I'm never going to give up on you."

Tears well up in my eyes. "Why not?"

"Because despite everything, I know you. I know your heart. And you are more than I ever could have imagined. You are the home I never knew I was looking for."

"I've never been someone's home," I whisper, tears spilling onto my cheeks.

A soft chuckle escapes him. "Silly woman. That's because you're mine."

I drag him down, desperation for physical connection overriding any panic that would have emerged from that statement. I want to show him what I'm not ready to voice yet.

That he's my home, too.

He meets me passion for passion until we're both panting and ripping at the last of his clothes.

I pause at the sight of him. I knew he was large from the outline in the sweatpants, but the man is actually massive. The largest I've seen by at least two inches.

He runs a hand over his cock, gathering the pre-cum at the tip and smoothing it down over the skin. "Something on your mind?"

"No wonder your ego is huge."

He barks a laugh, opposite hand roaming over my skin. "Appreciate it."

I pull him back down to me, fingernails digging into his shoulder blades as he teases me, slicking his cock with each slippery slide through my cunt. The very tip of his cock catches on my opening for just a moment before sliding past and bumping my clit again.

The palm of his hand smooths up the back of my thigh, pulling my leg up and against my chest. "Need me to put a condom on?"

I bite my lip at the way he slides again, electric hum zipping up my skin. "No. I'm on the pill."

"Thank fuck."

Instead of the dick he's been teasing me with, I get two fingers curled inside stroking the spot he discovered earlier. Every thrust takes me higher and further away from what I want.

"Just fuck me already, you teasing bastard!"

He just smiles, totally unaffected by my sass. Thankfully he obeys and removes his fingers, lining up with a hand on the base of his cock.

The initial push burns with how thick he is, and then . . . in a moment, my mind expands, and I can not only feel what I feel, but what Ash is feeling.

Fuck. What's happening?

The way my cunt wraps around him, how my fingers pull at his hair, how soft my skin is against his chest.

I feel everything.

"I wish you could see, baby. I wish you could see how fucking perfect we look together," he says, pushing a few more inches in.

The pain and pleasure melt together into a swirling flame that has me pushing my hips to force the rest of him inside me.

"Shit. Wait. C'mere." In a move I don't fully register, Ash pulls out, turns me around, and lifts me above his lap.

I open my eyes to a floor-length mirror. I'm in front hovering over Ash's glistening length, body taut and squirming. He's behind, his arm muscles bulging as he's holding me suspended.

"Watch while you take me, Goldilocks. Watch how perfectly we fit."

Slowly, he lines us up and lowers me onto him. He feels even bigger somehow from this angle, and I can't rip my eyes away from the sight of him disappearing inside me.

He's right. We look perfect.

"If only the whole world could see how stunning you are when you stretch around me. When you pull me in." He builds a steady rhythm, lifting me up and down as I surrender to the overwhelming pleasure. "If only everyone could see how completely you belong to me. No one would ever think to come near you again."

I wrap my hand around the back of his head as he bites at my neck, leaving marks I'll pretend to hate tomorrow.

The scent of sex fills the air, the sounds of our bodies and moans overwhelming the sounds of the world around us.

His fingers come down my chest and twirl around my clit, making my body jerk against his. "I wouldn't do that, though. God, I could never handle anyone seeing you like this. Promise me no one will."

I nod, knowing it's true. "Promise."

"Good girl. Now cum for me. For us."

I can only obey. My body erupts in orgasm, heat swirling through every inch of me until I scream. My orgasm triggers his, and the feel of it throws me into another, smaller orgasm.

Witchy shit for the win.

His hands smooth over me as we come down, anchoring me to him and to the present.

"Holy shit," I murmur, cum dripping onto the base of his cock and the blanket beneath us. "Holy fucking shit."

"You can say that again," he chuckles, breathless. He softly pulls out, both of us hissing at the action. "Let me take care of you. Bath?"

"Yeah."

He lays me back on the bed, brushing the hair off my face in an action that threatens to bring back the earlier tears. I can no longer ignore the devotion this man has for me.

Or the fact that no matter what I say, I'm shit at staying away from him.

The sounds of him puttering around the bathroom, running water for a bath, filter through the ajar door. I don't trust my legs yet to follow him in there, so I simply lie still, sweat and other things cooling on my skin.

ASH ROUSES me from the post-sex haze, lifting me into his arms. I wrap around his neck, burying my face into the soft skin there.

He carries me to the bathtub. It's a deep, large basin with actual clawfoots. I would guess—based on his size and everything else in this damn house—that it's a custom piece as well.

Without dropping me, he steps into the tub and sits with me still cradled in his arms. "How you feeling, Goldilocks?"

"Like I'm high."

He chuckles, turning me so his front is to my back. "I'll take that as a compliment. You set my plant on fire, by the way."

"I did *what*?!" I try to fly out of his arms, but he holds me tight. "What are you talking about?"

"Yeah, you set my plant on fire when you came. Luckily, being an Earth witch, it wasn't a problem for me to suppress it."

"How did I not notice a fucking plant on fire?"

Kind of badass, though. I don't want to risk burning down his house every time we have sex, but it's kind of cool that I did that.

His chest literally puffs up with pride. "I'm very good at what I do."

"Your ego didn't need the boost."

"Nothing to be done about it now. I'm officially boosted." He grabs a bar of soap—a kind I've seen sold at the market—and forms a lather in his hands. "Now let me finish looking after you and get us to bed."

I snuggle into his arms and let him clean me. It's soothing, somehow, letting him take care of me in this way.

I spent my life post-Dad fighting for scraps of affection. Mom spent all her energy fighting with Hazel, so she basically ignored me. Grandma was around once a month and did her best, but once a month isn't enough. Hazel was the one who gave me the most love, the most real safety.

But she was a child, and she wasn't prepared to give anyone what she herself barely got.

I've never found the validation, the love, I needed. I tried with boyfriends, with sex, with friends. It was never right.

Not until Ash.

This man who fights and fights and never gives up no matter how much I push him away. This man who sees me better than anyone else can.

He sees the outside I've so perfectly crafted to attract the attention I want, but he also sees the inside. The person who is hurt and trying to figure out what the fuck she's doing.

"I can't lose you," I whisper into the room, giving voice to the fear that has caused me to pull away from every single potential connection I've had. As desperately as I've craved love, I was so scared of losing it that I never let it grow.

His hands—which were lathering soap over my shoulders—still, turning me to face him. "Laura Hollis, I promise you won't."

"That's not a promise you can make."

He presses his forehead to mine. "I can't predict the future, no. But I can tell you right now that I'm not leaving you."

"I believe that," I concede.

"Do you want to tell me what's been going on in that beautiful head of yours? Or do you want me to make you cum again before we go to sleep and talk about it tomorrow?"

Despite everything, a soft giggle escapes me. "You're a menace, Ash Cedar."

"Your menace."

Mine. For the first time, I think I like the idea.

CHAPTER 23
SHOW ME

Sunlight filters through my closed eyelids as awareness tickles at me, waking me from the most restful sleep I can ever remember having. Warmth at my back has me snuggling toward it, pressing into hard muscles and soft skin.

Ash.

Right. We had mind-blowing sex and then got in bed, went for round two, and promptly fell asleep.

I wait for the panic to hit me. For the urge to dive for my clothes and run to my car.

Instead, safety washes over me like a gentle wave. Ash's arms are around me, holding me close and making me never want to leave.

Right now, I suppose I don't have to.

My eyes flit over what I can see of his room. It can't be too late, as the sunlight is still soft and hazy where it streams in from the window. The room itself isn't overly decorated, but there are photos of Ash and an older man. I'd guess it's his dad, if the resemblance is to be any indication.

They're relaxed, arms slung around each other in front of a young forest with small trees. Probably something they worked on together using magic. Their smiles are easy, and I think I should feel jealous. But all I feel is a warm sort of happiness that Ash has such a good relationship with his father.

And then there's the plant I set on fire. Sooty ash clinging to its branches.

I still can't fucking believe I did that and didn't even notice. Grandma would be oddly proud of me, I'm sure. I am, too.

"I can hear you thinking." Ash's morning voice is lower and rougher than usual and sends a sluice of heat down my spine.

"All good things," I reply honestly, pressing back into a few more inches of hardness that have awakened with Ash.

A soft groan is his response as he lines us up. He slowly grinds against my ass, one hand palming my breast.

I chuckle. "Seems you're thinking about something, too."

"I'm thinking you should always sleep naked," he says, other hand slipping down to collect the wetness that has gathered and twirl it around my clit. "I'm thinking waking up with you in my arms is the best goddamn thing I've ever experienced."

"Please," I whisper. How I can still be so hungry for him is astounding.

"Anything for you."

With a hand on his length, he guides himself to line up and pushes in from behind, keeping us spooning.

It happens again. The weirdest witchy thing I've ever experienced as I feel what he feels. What *we* feel.

"God, is it like this for you, too?" I ask, relishing the soft, lazy rhythm inspired by our soft, lazy morning.

He chuckles, fingers moving back and forth between my clit and where he spears me open. "I could never explain how good you feel."

"Flattering, but—" I gasp on a deeper thrust "—not exactly what I meant."

How do I explain it?

Lips fall to my neck, pressing softness to the bruises I caught sight of for a moment in the mirror last night. I won't be able to hide them, and I don't want to. I belong to someone, and the evidence of that on my skin is everything.

"I could spend the rest of my fucking life inside you," he says, panting in my ear like he just ran a marathon. "Tell me what you feel."

"You. Fuck, Ash, I feel *you.*"

His fingers still at the exact place his cock enters me. "That's me, Goldilocks, spearing you open. That's me filling you better than you've ever been filled. That's me staking my goddamn claim."

"*Oh,*" I gasp. I need him closer, I need more, I need. "Please turn me around. Please, I need to see you."

He pulls out, maneuvering me until I'm underneath all his broad muscles. His smiling face and shoulders block out the entire world in the best way. "I'm here, Laura."

I drag him down for a kiss, digging my nails into his back. The prickle of pain radiates in my skin as if it was *his* nails scraping my skin.

"I'd like to try something. May I?" he asks, eyes open and clear of any morning fatigue.

I nod. I trust him with everything I am, and everything I have.

A mischievous smirk twists his lips as he unwraps my arms from around his neck and presses them above my head.

Before I can say anything, vines slither in from the open window. They're slow, cautious, as if they're not sure how I'm going to react. They slip through the slats in the headboard and down until they wrap around my wrists.

"Sex magic?" I ask, testing my new bonds. "Who knew you had a kinky side."

"There's so much to me that you don't know yet," he practically growls, sliding back inside me in one confident thrust. "I can't wait to explore every single decadent thought I've ever had about you."

My legs circle around him, my heels digging into his toned ass. "Show me."

His speed picks up, sweat making his abs glisten in the morning light. This perfect person is all mine.

I struggle against the bonds, wanting to sink my fingers in his hair or leave more crescent moons on his back. But not being able to makes it hotter. The resistance. The desire left unfulfilled.

He lifts my thigh, bringing my leg up to rest against his shoulder. It changes the angle, causing the very tip of him to hit that miraculous spot that nothing other than my big purple dildo had found until Ash.

My back arches underneath him, the hard points of my nipples scraping against his chest. I moan his name, surrendering to the onslaught of pleasure.

"I could survive on the way you say my name alone." He's close, he's so close and I'm almost there. "I could feast on your sounds for the rest of my life and be sated."

"Please," I whimper. I'm not sure exactly what it is I need, but I know I need it. "Please, Ash."

"I'll tell you once, I'll tell you a million times. I've got you, Laura Hollis," he says, emerald eyes peering into my soul. His thumb slips and slides against my clit, the slick between us making his calluses glide like silk. "And I'm yours."

Fireworks spark behind my eyes as my orgasm slams into me with the force of a thousand fiery suns exploding at the same time. It drags me under, his own orgasm heightening mine and threatening to make me lose consciousness.

Slowly, the intensity ebbs until I'm left with his weight pressing on me, and free hands to wind around his shoulders.

"Can we spend every morning like this?" he asks, lifting his head to show me his goofy smile.

Fondness melts any lingering defenses until I'm grinning just as goofily. "Pretty sure it would be too much for you. You're not getting any younger."

"I'm twenty-seven."

I suck in a breath. "That old, huh?"

He shrugs, bracketing my head with his forearms. God, they're so fucking thick. "You like it."

"Women across history have ignored much worse things than age for good dick."

"So you admit I have good dick?"

I level him with a heavy stare. "As much as I truly don't believe your ego needs feeding, it would be ridiculous to try and lie about how good that was."

"My woman is so goddamn romantic."

I boop him on the nose. "And don't you forget it."

He laughs—loud and boisterous and free. The sound makes me yearn for that level of levity and lightness. Makes me want to fix things with Hazel and be better.

Ash Cedar is going to make me a better person. How utterly horrid.

"Shower with me and I'll drop you off at the market," he says, pushing himself onto his knees.

I sigh heavily. "I can't just stay in bed all day?"

"Goldilocks, I'll keep you in bed for the rest of your days if you want me to."

Part of me does want to lock myself away in Ash's lumberjack tree house kingdom. But I can't.

Giving Hazel some space after last night was smart, but abandoning Grandma's booth at the market isn't.

"Shower and market," I reluctantly agree, sitting up.

He stands, offering me his hand. "You're not alone anymore. Whatever it is you don't want to face, you won't do it by yourself."

I launch myself into his arms, burying my face in his chest.

I'm not alone anymore.

CHAPTER 24
THE ARMCHAIR IS HORRID

It's hell not having Ash at my side, but Hazel, Grandma, and I don't need an audience. We need to have this conversation alone.

The house welcomes me with a creaking hello. I like to think it missed me, but just because it's slightly sentient doesn't mean it has emotions.

Right?

Voices drift in from the open door to the backyard. It's winter, you dummies, why is the door open?

I step through the living room, approaching the door, and the heat emanating from it is intense. Why in the world is it so hot? I tip-toe quietly to get a better look.

They better not have contacted a Fire witch without telling me.

There, in the center of the backyard, is a bonfire like I've never seen. Layers and layers of crisscrossed logs stand what has to be five feet high. All engulfed in flame.

As if it recognizes me, the fire cracks at my arrival outside. The smoke billows toward me. Welcoming me.

"I'm burning the negative energy this family has accumulated. I'm hoping the smoke of it clears your lungs enough to say what is on your minds," Grandma announces from next to the pyre. "That, and I'm sick of the armchair in the guest room. It's horrid."

True to fact, an armchair sits on the very top.

"I told her this would give us lung cancer," Hazel grouses from the other side. Decidedly downwind from the billowing plumes.

The smile on Ash's father's face from the photo I saw in Ash's bedroom flits through my mind. "Cancer isn't a punchline."

"That's not what I—" Hazel's face is stricken.

I shake my head. It was a cheap shot. "I know. I shouldn't have said that."

"There's a lot left unsaid here," Grandma says. "Some of that is my fault, a majority of that is your mother's, and a lot of that is both of yours." She holds a hand up to prevent the responses that are on the tips of both mine and Hazel's tongues. "You're adults now. You're not responsible for the trauma of your upbringing, but addressing it and not repeating the same mistakes? That *is* your responsibility."

That shuts us up. She's not wrong and there isn't really anything else to be said about it.

Grandma stands taller. "I'm on the waitlist for a family therapist, but just like in the human world, our therapists have long waitlists. So in the meantime, I was hoping we could at least open the door to better communication."

Well, damn, Grandma. Someone has been putting in work.

The fire catches my attention again. I've never been around this much at one time, and my heart is practically leaping toward it.

"I'll start," Hazel says, taking a deep breath. "I have some resentment for having to be a parent when I was a kid. It's hard for me to separate my anger and I'm sorry for saying what I did last night."

I should be paying attention. I know she's saying something I need to hear, but the whispering. The whispering is so much louder. So insistent.

Help.

"What help do you need?" I ask, stepping closer to the flame. "Who are you?"

Help me.

"Who are you?" I ask again, holding a hand as close to the fire as I can without burning it.

Laura?

For the first time, I recognize the voice. I know that slightly judgmental lilt, that defensive tone. I make sense of the whispers, and it's worse than I ever imagined.

"Mom." Even as I say it, I can't believe it. I knew she wasn't dead, I knew it. But being able to hear her through fire? That's not good. It can't be good.

"Mom? What are you talking about?" Hazel's yanking me away from the fire, but I can barely feel her touch. Her voice is a soft melody a million miles away.

I'm sorry. I'm so sorry.

"Where are you?" I yell at her, voice shaking with emotion. "How do I find you?"

I'm left unanswered. The connection is broken. I'm in my yard, with my sister and my grandma; they stare at me as if they've seen a ghost.

Lucky them. I've actually spoken to one. I may have started moving on with my life, but Mom found a way to fuck it all up again.

My eyes burn with tears as I try to wrap my head around this. If only I could have kept the connection up longer. Why couldn't I? Where is she?

"Come," Grandma whispers, taking my hand in hers. "Come inside, dear."

～

"HERE, DEAR. DRINK THIS."

Grandma stuffs a warm mug in my hands, but nothing compares to the heat of the fire. The lick of the flames.

Everything else is cold in comparison.

I lift the concoction to my lips, wrinkling my nose at the smell. "What the hell is in this?"

"Best not to ask about Grandma's teas. They usually taste awful—no offense—but do exactly what you need them to," Hazel says. She's a solid fifteen feet away from me and I can tell it's not because I smell.

It's because of what I said.

Her arms hug around herself as if trying to build a wall against whatever the hell she's feeling. Fear, if I had to guess, based on the way her eyes keep darting around. She's like a deer in the woods, easily spooked and careful.

"Now, if you can, tell us what happened," Grandma says. Her voice is calm, but she can't hide the terror in her eyes. The what-the-fuck energy we're all feeling.

Bitter fluid slides over my tongue and I do my best not to spit it out. However it tastes, I'm sure it's worth it.

I clear my throat of the ball of emotion lodged inside. "I could hear Mom."

Hazel gasps, clutching herself even tighter.

"At first, it was just a voice asking for help. But then the voice said my name; it called me Laura. I knew it was Mom. How could I not? She apologized and then I lost her."

"You lost her?" Grandma asks, hand on mine. She grips me too tight, her eyes wild. But I don't ask her to let go.

I nod. "I couldn't hear her anymore. I wasn't connected anymore."

"How is this possible?" Hazel whispers. "We watched her get devoured in a Hell-destined ball of water with an obsessed warlock."

"She needs help." I squeeze Grandma in return. She has to believe me. "We have to help Mom."

"I haven't heard of something like this before," Grandma says.

It's unsettling that I've found the one thing she hasn't seen—she prides herself on never being surprised by anything.

"Are we really considering the possibility Mom is—what—alive and trapped in Hell?" Hazel asks, throwing her hands up in the air.

Frustration boils over. "Are you calling me a fucking liar?"

Before Hazel can open her mouth, the front door bangs open. It jumps on the hinges and slams against the wall. The house groans in reply, annoyed at the slight damage that probably did.

Ash stands there, head swiveling until he meets my gaze. "There you are."

I shouldn't immediately want to jump his bones. But damn, the protectiveness in this man's eyes does things to me.

He strides over with confidence, with purpose. I'm the purpose.

"Are you okay? You disappeared for a few minutes. Literally disappeared, as if you weren't here anymore, and I've never felt —" he cuts himself off by pressing a kiss to my forehead. He lingers after, pressing his nose to the top of my head. "Scared the shit out of me."

"I'm okay," I reply. Has anyone given this much of a damn about me before?

Grandma hums. "Seems I was right all along."

I glare at her from around Ash's hulking form, but it does nothing. Despite her words, both her and Hazel are staring at me with mouths open. They've never seen me like this with someone before.

"Believe me now, Hazel?" I ask, trying to distance them from Ash and my closeness with him. "I was talking to Mom in Hell and that's why Ash couldn't feel me."

"You did *what?*" Ash rears back. "What now?"

Hazel sighs. "It's not that I thought you were lying, I promise. It's just . . . beyond anything I ever thought possible. I've been trying to mourn her . . . and . . . I don't know how to process any of this!"

I deflate. I have to learn to stop picking at her. We were so good at being sisters for so many years. It's ridiculous that a handful of months have destroyed all that.

"We can talk about this when you're done?" Ash asks. He's probably worried, but he's being that safe calmness in the storm that he always seems to be.

"Wait for me upstairs."

He presses another kiss to the top of my head and goes for the stairs.

"Second door on the right!" I call after him absentmindedly. I completely spaced on the fact he's never been inside the house before.

The silence that follows is deep, deafening in the absence of any noise. Even the house doesn't know what to do.

"Mom is alive?" Hazel finally breaks the silence.

I nod, something in me knowing the answer before she even finishes asking. "She is. Whether Draven is using his magic to keep her alive, or she's using her own, she's alive. And she needs our help."

A tear slips down Grandma's cheek, but she can't form words. Not yet.

And I don't blame her. Grandma and Mom have barely seemed related, let alone mother and daughter, but I can't imagine how Grandma's feeling.

"So we'll help her," I say. "We'll help her because despite all the shit she put us through, she doesn't deserve to suffer in Hell at the hands of Draven."

Hazel's cheeks are wet, and she doesn't protest.

There's nothing more to discuss tonight. We need time to process before we untangle these emotions.

But Ash? Ash deserves a conversation.

Anxiety grows around the room like vines around a tree. It's practically growing out of the walls by the time I close my bedroom door behind me.

His feelings are valid. Repeating that to myself does nothing to quell the defensiveness sliding up my skin.

"Please. Explain to me what's going on." His request isn't unreasonable. He deserves that, at the very least.

I sigh. Where the hell do I even begin?

Actually, Hell is probably a good place to start.

"Do you remember the daemon incident at the market? When my sister was attacked?"

He nods. I bite my lip at the way his forearms bulge as he crosses them.

"His name was Botis, and he was sent by a warlock named Draven. Draven and my mom apparently had some sort of affair—the details are murky—before she met my dad. And whatever it is ended when she met him, because my dad was her soulmate. This pissed off the warlock, because of course it did, and he decided to make her pay. So she banished his brother to Hell, *he* killed our dad, and *she's* been hunting his family. Although the details on that are murky too, because I don't think any of them are his blood relatives. But whatever. And then he kidnapped Noah—that's Hazel's human soulmate—so we went to a meetup Draven set up. And Mom dissolved her and Draven in a giant water bubble. We've been assuming she's dead, but I didn't really think she was because the fire told me she wasn't. And tonight the fire was so big and unfiltered and I could finally hear it. Really hear it. And it was her, and she's alive so now we have to go get her." I exhale a heavy breath. I may need a drink after that.

Ash blinks. Blinks again.

Opens his mouth to speak, then shuts it. Blinks once more instead.

"It's a lot." I twirl a lock of blonde hair between my fingers. Ugh. I have to stop doing that. It's a nervous habit and I look like a worried child when I do it.

In a moment, he's across the room and I'm buried in his arms. One hand is splayed across my lower back, the other tangled in my hair.

Both pressing me impossibly close.

"I am so fucking sorry, Laura."

It's the use of my first name in this way that pisses me off. "I don't want your pity. I don't need it."

He pulls back, forcing me to meet his gaze. "I'm not pitying you, Goldilocks, I'm telling you I'm fucking sorry."

That's almost worse.

He presses the sweetest, softest kiss to the top of my head, and it hammers at the cracks in my heart so hard that they all splinter.

Sobs wrack my body, leaving me heaving and gasping into his t-shirt. Every single tear I've kept locked inside since my mom disappeared, since Hazel left, since Dad died, is determined to finally be free.

And I can't stop it.

"Come here," Ash says, lifting me into a bridal carry. He lays me down on my bed, takes off my shoes, and settles in beside me.

His arms hold me until his shirt is soaked to the bone and I have nothing left. Until my breaths even out and I have nothing left.

Until I hear him whisper, "I love you, Laura Hollis, and I'll be your safe place until the day I die."

CHAPTER 25

SHE LOVES YOU

I can't sleep.

Not with Mom's 'I'm sorry' ringing in my head. Not with Ash telling me he loves me. My head is full of fireflies, lighting up and buzzing around until I can't sit still anymore.

It may be three a.m., but there's no way I can just keep lying here. Despite Ash being the most comfortable human heated blanket on the planet.

I walk along the cold wood floors with bare feet, which sends shivers up my spine. No socks in winter was a very bad idea.

Eventually, I reach my destination. Mom's room.

No one—to my knowledge—has been in here since Mom vanished. Granted, I don't think I've ever actually been in her room at all.

There were no lazy mornings snuggling together as a family in our mom's bed, no hair braiding on the comforter, no book reading.

That all happened in Hazel's room, just the two of us.

Every nightmare was Hazel's to soothe. Every late-night chat was hers. Every lazy morning.

She's my family, and she's the person I'm the furthest from right now.

I open the door. It makes a noisy creak of disuse, and I shush the house. "People are sleeping!"

The door quiets, but not without a sassy groan in reply.

The décor is plain, and a thin layer of dust coats everything, but that's not surprising.

What's surprising is how many photos of Dad litter the surfaces. Old frames, new frames, some just left loose on the dresser. There are no pictures of him anywhere in the house. I thought maybe she'd burned them all or cried over them so much they were warped and unrecognizable.

But no. She hoarded them in her sacred space and didn't share them. Let us believe there weren't any left.

My heart pangs at the betrayal. Maybe she doesn't deserve to be saved.

Maybe she deserves whatever hell she's burning in.

I lift the closest frame. It's of Dad standing on the front porch, a camera of his own hanging lazily at his side. I forgot how big his smile was. I forgot about the little gray wisps at his temples.

I forgot how much Hazel resembles him.

Same auburn hair and facial structure. She has his nose and his brow.

A flare of jealousy rises in my gut. I wish so desperately that I had a piece of him of my own.

I snap the back of the frame, pulling the photo out and pocketing it.

The house creaks at me, nudging me along.

I trail my fingers through the dust as I look at every photo. So many of them are of Dad with one of us—either Mom, me, or Hazel. Only the one I took is of him alone.

The last photo is on Mom's bedside table. And it has no dust.

Strange.

But there's something there. A folded-up piece of paper right underneath the photo. I pull it gently, nerves skittering up my arm. I don't know why but this feels . . . It feels important.

I open it up and see Mom's handwriting. Her doctor-level

chicken scratch that I always wanted to tease her for, but she couldn't be bothered to even look at me most days.

She wasn't like Grandma or Hazel, she didn't understand that teasing is my way of showing love.

Hazel and Laura,

I'm so sorry. If you're reading this, it's because I banished both myself and Draven to Hell and I'm no longer here with you. You're probably very confused, and that's understandable. I haven't been much of a mother to either of you, and I've left you with more questions than answers. Losing your father broke me in ways I never thought possible. I've never been able to fix it. Fix me.

My sacrifice will save Noah and will stop Hazel from feeling the brokenness that ruined everything I hold dear. I haven't done much right, but I know that I can't have one of you feeling this way.

And let's be honest. I may have technically been alive all this time, but I stopped living a long time ago. The fact that I've been forced to continue on all this time is going to mean something now, and that gives me peace.

I'm sorry.

Mom

My sniffles cut through the silence.

I don't know if I'll ever truly forgive her, but this? Knowing she had planned to do this to protect Hazel? Some of the wall I've constructed around my mother cracks.

Maybe she changed a little before she died. Maybe the person she is now can change.

I pocket the letter alongside the photo of Dad. It's addressed to both Hazel and me but I don't know if I'm ready to share it. I don't know if she's ready to see it.

She hates Mom so much, and a lot of that is justified. And the rift between her and me is so deep.

I just don't know what I want to do yet.

Right next to the letter is a small box, no bigger than the palm of my hand. It's an old thing, potentially passed down from Grandma. Or at the very least, found at an antique store.

The lid squeaks a little—just like the door—as I lift it. Sitting in the middle, on a plush bed of red velvet, is a compact. Small, with gold detailing in the shape of water droplets.

It looks custom made, something connected to her element and herself. It's beautiful.

It's something I would love to have learned how to make.

I open the latch and look back at my own face. Of course it's a mirror, but that's not what stops me. It's how different I look.

Before Hazel left, I could point out all the places that were fake. All the many points of my face and body that I had spent hours crafting to attract the type of attention I wanted. Needed. The meticulous makeup, the fashionable outfits, the come-hither smirk and doe eyes.

This person? Despite how fucked up I still am, this person looks so much more authentically me. My hair is a sexed-up mess, my eyes are bright and alive—if not a little tear-filled—and my skin is clear and glowing.

This person is more Laura Hollis than I've ever felt.

I pocket the compact with the letter and photograph, turning my back on the room.

~

I WAKE BEFORE ASH, despite being up for most of the night, and it's easy to pretend I don't need to deal with everything that happened in Mom's room yet.

It's also easy to prioritize caffeine over everything else when you're as drained as I am. The warm scent of French press leads me to the kitchen. Not my first choice, but irresistible in this moment.

Noah is there, preparing two cups, and he looks up at my approach.

We're the only people awake in the house, and by the look on his face I am the absolute last person he wants to see.

"Hey," he says cautiously, as if I might snap at him.

"I'm sorry for the other night," I reply. May as well rip the Band-Aid off, and I am sorry. I'm just not ready to say it to Hazel yet.

He exhales a large breath, shoulders lowering in relief. I'm not surprised he expected a fight. He hasn't really seen the best of me.

He passes me with steaming mugs in hand as I head toward the cupboard. "She loves you a lot, you know." Noah's words stop me dead. "Hazel loves you so much. She just . . . The way your mom raised the both of you sounds like absolute shit. And she struggles with how to be a sister to you after . . . you know." His hand waves a little in what I'm assuming is reference to his kidnapping and Mom.

I nod, unable to do more in reply. With a smile, he's back on his way upstairs.

Our dynamic was thrown on its head when she left, and knowing Mom is alive? RIP our sanity.

I should probably bring Ash some coffee. If I had to guess, he's either a massive sugar junkie or takes it completely black.

No in between.

Noah made some peppermint coffee thing that smells like Christmas and I'm practically salivating over it by the time I make it back to my room.

"That smells fucking delicious," Ash growls from underneath

a mountain of pillows he's managed to burrow under in my absence. His head pops up. "And I don't just mean the coffee."

"How are you managing to be charming when you're barely awake? Please don't tell me you're a morning person."

Morning people are a specific breed of weird.

He chuckles, diving back into his soft fortress. "M'not usually. But I can't help it when you're around."

"Ugh, shut up."

Despite my words I crawl back into bed with him, leaning against the cream fabric headboard.

It's entirely domestic, really. Waking up slowly together with a cup of coffee in a warm bed.

"Do you want to talk about what happened last night?" Ash asks, sitting up with me and grabbing the extra cup.

"Not really. But I'm assuming you're probably worried?"

He huffs a laugh with no humor. "I'm not a huge fan of the fact that you've been communicating with Hell, no. And I'd like to know what the plan is."

"That makes two of us," I mutter, taking a sip. It's Christmas in a cup. Peppermint and chocolate and coffee all swirled together like the best candy cane.

"Just talk to me, Goldilocks." He places his hand on my thigh over the covers. "And we'll figure it out."

I close my eyes, leaning my head back. How do I even begin to process all that's happened, and all that's now changed?

I attempted to last night and look where that got me. Sobbing like an idiot until Ash fell asleep and then roaming the house like some sort of dramatic ghost.

Listen, crying is great. Super awesome. Release those emotions, burn those calories. But not like that. Not like what I did.

That was beyond.

"I don't really have much of a choice, do I? I have to learn how to communicate fully with Mom so I can find out where she is, and we can figure out how to go get her. As far as a plan? I don't know enough about all this magic junk to have any idea."

He scratches at his beard. "I can't say I have a lot of experience with this either. And I haven't heard anything about it. I could ask my dad, but I'd be surprised if he knows much more than I do."

"I have a feeling it's a *unique* situation."

And I also have a feeling unique doesn't begin to cover it.

CHAPTER 26

DYSFUNCTIONAL AS THEY COME

Grandma asks for some time to ask around about Hell, and she gathers us for a normal family dinner a week later. For that week I spent each night at Ash's house being fucked against every surface he's ever imagined.

Turns out the guy has a pretty vivid imagination.

And it's the best kind of distraction.

Belle is also loving being around Ash. For a guy who claims to be more of a dog person, he certainly spoils the shit out of her. That's the main reason she's still there even though I'm at home.

Treats trump chosen witch every time, apparently.

I drop my overnight bag—which has really been an over-week bag—onto the floor in the foyer. While I'm not opposed to wearing no underwear, I really should swap and wash.

"Hey," Hazel says softly from the couch. She and I haven't spoken since the night of the bonfire. Not because I'm actively avoiding her, but because I don't think either of us know what to say to each other.

And I like to think we don't want a repeat of our fight.

"Hey. Grandma here?" I ask, walking into the living room.

The room is dominated by the giant-ass portrait of our family over the fireplace. It's gaudy and large and, honestly, we all look constipated in it. Dad spent the entire time making faces at Hazel and I trying to get us to laugh. He always knew how to make the most mundane activities fun.

The wrong parent died that day.

A tear slips down my cheek. What kind of person thinks something like that? Especially after reading what Mom put in her letter. I thought I was changing, but maybe that slick, oily, angry part of my soul will always be there.

"She's at the shop, said she'd be back soon." Hazel leans toward me. "Are you okay, Laura?"

Nope. Not even close.

"Of course. Why wouldn't I be?" I flip my hair over my shoulder and sit across from her on the floral armchair.

She shakes her head but doesn't fight me.

Maybe it's petty, but why do I have to be the one who's vulnerable first? Why is it me that has to put their shit on the line? It's not like she's over there offering up her insecurities and deepest fears.

Why does Noah have to tell me more about how she feels than she will?

Thankfully the door opens, and Grandma's lavender-and-smoke scent fills the house. The woman burns so much incense it's practically soaked into her skin.

"Hello girls!" she says, shucking off her winter coat. "I picked up Chinese!"

The fact she's so cheery should calm me, relax me, but it doesn't. It feels like overcompensating, and I immediately don't trust it.

Lo Mein is High Trouble.

We're immediately on our feet and setting up for dinner. It's one of those well-oiled moments that only comes from years of familiarity. We all know who grabs the dishes, the silverware, the drinks. Things have changed a little since Mom, though. She was the one who plated dinner, but now Grandma does that. Dad used to put on music. Now we eat in silence.

We're a family. Dysfunctional as they come.

"Have you learned anything?" I finally ask after the appetizers of spring rolls and potstickers have been devoured and we're well on our way through our main courses.

Good food can only distract me for so long.

"Not much, yet. I have a few meetings this week though, and I'll share what I know after dinner," Grandma replies.

Annoyance buzzes around my head like little bees. Considering I'm the one who actually communicated with Mom, shouldn't I be in these meetings? It makes me feel a little better knowing that Hazel has been covering the shop completely to allow Grandma to make her rounds. She's not involved either.

HOT COCOA with marshmallows and chocolate sprinkles warms my fingers as I hold the mug close to my chest. Grandma finishes off her tea before joining us in the living room, and the house creaks in an ominous way.

Like a warning.

"I'm sorry if I've drawn this out, girls." Grandma glides into the room. "As I said before, I haven't found out too much yet. Fire witches are so rare that nailing one down for a conversation is difficult, and they are generally a secretive bunch on top of that."

I preen a little. Part of me likes being unique.

"So you called a family meeting to tell us you don't have any information?" I snark. And everyone says I'm the dramatic one.

"I was not finished." Grandma holds me with her gaze, daring me to oppose her. "Despite there not being much information available, I have set up a meeting with a Fire witch that Dotty knows in a couple weeks. I'd like you both to join me."

"Weeks?" My mouth drops open. "That's practically forever! Mom needs help now."

"I couldn't get her to agree to anything earlier with the holidays coming up. We're just going to have to get past the new year," Grandma says, resignation in her tone.

Hazel huffs a little. "Mom can wait a second. If we're doing this, we're not going in blind. I would rather have all the information and do this rescue right the first time."

She's not wrong, but the disregard for Mom makes me bristle. I get it, though. She hasn't seen the letter. I don't know how to tell her about it. I don't know how to tell her anything.

"Between now and then we will resume magic lessons and hone your craft. And I would encourage the two of you to have a real conversation. You were making progress the other night and got interrupted. Our family therapy sessions should start soon." Grandma sits taller. "I got us bumped up the list after last week."

Nothing like hearing your mother begging you for a rescue from Hell to get a therapist to take you more seriously.

Hazel and I both nod, but don't say anything else. I have a feeling it will be radio silence until we get into therapy.

As usual.

CHAPTER 27
FAMILY TRAUMA

The clock tick-tock-ticks in the corner as we sit in silence. Discomfort falls on us like a layer of dirt while being buried alive.

We're in the office of Dr. Penelope Farrow, witch-family therapist only a few days later. She made us a 'special priority.'

Dr. Farrow clears her throat, her black bob tickling her chin. "Does anyone have anything in particular they'd like to address first?"

I snort. Where the fuck do we even begin?

Grandma smooths her muumuu, bangles jangling on her wrist. "We've had a lot of trauma as a family. For many years, and we've needed to address it."

"It's a big step to seek out therapy, especially with how much stigma still surrounds it. You're allowed to be proud of this step," Dr. Farrow says.

This entire thing is going to kill me. The only reason I'm here is because Ash encouraged it. Told me over and over about how wonderful therapy has been for him and how it could really help fix things between me and Hazel. How much he'd love to have a sibling to lean on for help during his dad's cancer treatment.

He was naked while he said it, which heavily influenced how much I was listening to him, if I'm honest.

Ash could ask me to do anything while he was naked, and I'd probably do it. Stupid pretty abs.

"We lost a member of our family recently," Grandma says. "My daughter. Their mother. And we've just now learned she's not gone after all, and she needs our help. It's a bit to process."

"Did you have enough time to start the grieving process? Accept that she may really be gone just for the rug to be ripped out from underneath you?" Dr. Farrow's pen zooms across the paper, writing notes on all our dysfunction. The fun part? She's not holding it. A branch from the small potted tree in the corner is controlling the pen.

Grandma nods. "At least, Hazel and I did. Laura always had a feeling things weren't what they seemed—Laura's the one who figured it out, actually."

Thanks for the spotlight, Grandma. I was kind of hoping to slip through here unnoticed for the first time in my life.

Dr. Farrow turns her gaze to me, watching me with beady brown eyes behind thick glasses. "It must've felt vindicating to show your family that your feeling was correct."

I see your trap, lady.

"They didn't feel what I felt, and I don't hold that against them. Why wouldn't they start grieving?" Lie number one of the day. Of course I hold it against them.

They didn't believe me, just like they never believe me.

I'm Laura—the silly, airheaded, bitchy one who never has anything of true value to contribute.

"Because you warned them. Why wouldn't they believe you?" Dr. Farrow is relentless. Like a dog with a bone.

I cross my arms. "I don't know, Dr. Farrow. Why wouldn't they?"

A small smile graces her lips. It's not condescending . . . Maybe amused? Like she's appreciating that I'm not making this easy for her or something. Maybe she likes a challenge.

"Why don't we all drink some tea as we contemplate what Laura just shared?" Dr. Farrow waves her hand and another branch emerges, lifting a tray from the little kitchenette and bringing it toward us.

We're in her house. Apparently most witch therapists do their work from their homes. Something about the healing energy grounding them.

The branch places the tray on the little wooden coffee table in front of the couch, and Dr. Farrow encourages us with a gentle nod.

Grandma takes the first sip, delicately sniffing it first. It must be deemed safe as she grins and relaxes back against the cushions. Hazel picks up her mug after watching to make sure it was okay.

"I'm an Earth witch, first and foremost. I use my talent with emotions to infuse my herbs with healing and safety. It helps to open your heart to tough discussions," Dr. Farrow explains, obviously noticing my hesitation.

Definitely not drinking that, then.

"It makes sense that Laura would think we didn't believe her. And maybe we didn't. But it wasn't that we didn't believe her because we thought she was wrong, it's more that we couldn't put hope into the idea that she could be right," Hazel says, sipping the tea.

They'd have to hold me down and force that truth juice down my throat. My mug stays on the tray, softly steaming.

"We have a complicated relationship with our mother. She's a tough subject all around, but the thought that she didn't really die? My brain couldn't process it." Hazel's eyebrows raise as if she's surprised that came out of her mouth.

"So what I'm hearing is that while it would be perfectly natural for Laura to take that rejection personally, it was more that you were rejecting the idea itself? Not Laura's intuition?" Dr.

Farrow's pen is still wildly scratching along. We're going to give this woman enough content for a book.

Hazel nods. "I guess so? Yeah."

Everyone turns to me as if I'm supposed to respond to this.

"Cool?" I shrug.

Dr. Farrow chuckles. "I'm guessing therapy wasn't your idea, Laura."

"How did you ever come to that conclusion?"

Grandma slaps my arm lightly. I'm probably embarrassing her by being rude. Holding up the honor of the Pruitt name in public is real big with her.

"You're more likable than you'd like to believe," Dr. Farrow says, winking at me. "And you're also not required to participate if you aren't ready. We can focus on everyone else's feelings about Sarah—I believe that's what you said her name was over the phone—and her potentially being part of your lives again."

Works for me.

"I don't know if I do want her back in our lives," Hazel says. Now that her words are flowing, she's apparently unable to stop. "I don't want her in Hell, and I'll do everything I can to get her out. But let's be honest. The woman is toxic, and I don't want her drowning us again with her bullshit. I feel like we've only just now been able to start breathing again."

Bold to talk shit about Grandma's own daughter in front of her, but go off, sis.

Grandma's head drops, eyes falling to the mug sitting in her lap. But she doesn't say a word.

Guess that truth tea doesn't work on other Earth witches.

"That's an entirely valid way to feel about someone who has mistreated you. It's easy to write someone off when they're no one, but your own mother? That comes with familial guilt and a sense of loyalty that she may not entirely deserve. It's very coura-geous that you still want to save her, but the role she has in your life once she's saved is entirely your decision." Dr. Farrow's words draw a gasp out of all three of us. "Just because she's a member of your family doesn't mean you owe her anything. Especially if she herself hasn't done anything to earn that."

Tears well up in Hazel's eyes. She's trembling and my fingers itch to wrap around hers.

But I don't let them.

"Boundaries are important. We respect others' and we respect our own. Your boundary may be that you don't want her in your life. Someone else sitting here may choose differently. And that's okay."

What would happen if Hazel cut Mom off completely again? The first time that happened, it practically ruined our relationship for good. While we're definitely not in a good place, at least we're speaking.

Sort of.

That's more than I can say for us just a few months ago.

"I think," Dr. Farrow continues, "it would be good for you to focus on the three of you as a family over the holiday season. Whichever holiday you celebrate, put thought into your presents and be intentional with your time. Show each other how much love there is in this family still. And then, once the new year comes, figure out how to save Sarah. Maybe strengthening that bond will allow you to find a way to support one another in this endeavor."

Christmas is in a week, isn't it?

For someone who loves shopping, I really lost track of fucking time. I haven't gotten anything for anyone.

Including Ash. Do I get something for Ash? Of course I should.

Probably.

He's my boyfriend-soulmate-thing.

I mentally check out of therapy and put together a bullet list in my head. This is going to suck.

CHAPTER 28

CHRISTMAS SHOPPING

I pull my fuzzy hood further over my head as I trample through the slush and snow in the market the next day.

I have to figure out Christmas presents for these bitches, and the market is the best place to start. Even if there are fewer booths than ever now that the snow is really coming down.

Gotta love that Northeast Ohio snow.

Not.

Okay, the therapist told me to be thoughtful and express my love with these gifts. Because showing emotion is totally my strong suit.

Absolutely.

My relationship with Grandma is probably the least volatile. She and I are on pretty reasonable terms, so that seems like a safe place to start. To work the shopping muscle and get it warmed up for the harder ones.

Grandma enjoys books, muumuus, tea, herbs, gossiping, and other Earth witch things like cooking and gardening.

I keep my eyes peeled as I walk along the booths, trying to find anything that screams Grandma.

Huh. I slow my slightly frustrated gait to a full stop.

A vintage tea set draws me in. It has a floral motif, with red roses decorating the four porcelain cups, matching plates, and teapot. It's something she would use—something she would like.

The little sticker says it's in my price range, miraculously.

I haggle with the woman behind the booth and cross the easiest purchase off my list.

Now on to Hazel. Fuck.

What does Hazel like? Being a martyr. Maybe I can get her a cross.

Okay, no, I'm not that much of a bitch.

She's an artist. Enjoys all manner of art supplies and artwork. She has horrible clothes. I really should buy the woman an entirely new wardrobe. Maybe get her a haircut, too. The way some layers would do her facial structure wonders . . .

I'm getting sidetracked.

Presents. Focus.

A sparkle from my left catches my eye. I turn toward it, moving closer almost against my will.

It's a necklace. A locket with a paintbrush etched into the silver.

"There's a protection spell on that," a woman says, appearing to my right. I almost jump at her sudden materialization. "A very powerful, ancient one. Physical manifestations of the spell are inside the locket."

"How much of that is true and how much is you trying to make a sale?" I ask her, raising a brow. She's not the typical old crone you'd expect to say something like that, which I'll give her points for. She's around Mom's age, with long black hair braided into a gorgeous tail down her back.

She laughs. "I respect a bit of healthy disbelief. It's very true, but even if you don't believe it—it's still a pretty necklace."

Hazel has been protecting me all my life—even as angry as I am, I can admit that. Something about protecting her feels right.

"I'll take it."

∽

"WELL, aren't you a sight for sore eyes, Goldilocks?" Ash says, coming up behind me.

Busted. Not me looking at fucking wood-splitting axes because I have no fucking idea what to get him.

Who knew he'd be a harder buy than Hazel?

"Can I help you?" I try for sass, but the last word leaves my mouth in a whine as Ash moves in front of me, wrapping his large hand around the back of my neck and into my hair.

He pulls just a smidge to lift my gaze to his, that always indulgent smile on his face. "I can think of a few things you could help me with, actually."

"I'm busy." I try to clear the buzzy desire from my head. "While I understand that you could never get enough of how amazing I am, I do have a life."

"I miss you, too," he chuckles. "What are you doing?"

He squeezes the back of my neck and retreats, wrapping his arm around my waist instead. The hold is loose but still possessive, as if he enjoys others seeing us twisted together.

"Christmas shopping. Which is why it is a *solo* activity."

"We're only a week out—cutting it pretty close there, aren't you?" His deep green eyes pull me in just like they always do.

"I'm supposed to believe you've already bought all your presents?"

"Of course I have. I couldn't go two days this entire month without seeing something that reminded me of you somehow."

Soft, gooey affection warms my heart. It's official. The man is too good for me.

"I excel at shopping for myself." We move away from the axes that were absolutely a horrible idea. "Not for others."

"I know you well enough now to know that you excel at everything you do. But I don't need any gifts—I finally got you to admit that you're head over heels for me." His smile is smug. "I'm good."

I huff. "Does having an ego that size ever get unbearably heavy?"

"I don't know, Goldilocks. Does it?"

It's annoying having a partner who isn't afraid of you in the slightest. Who meets you blow for verbal blow and doesn't let you hide behind the coping mechanisms that have kept you safe for years.

"For what it's worth," he continues, "I don't think you have an ego. I think you're confident and strong, and I admire the fuck out of you."

That statement absolutely doesn't make my eyes burn.

"What sort of things do you like doing when you're not chopping wood, fucking me, or stealing my cat's affection?" I bulldoze through the emotional moment.

"Belle does love me, doesn't she?" His smile is large and genuine, full of affection for the little animal who chose me above anyone else. And I smile in return. "I don't have a whole lot of time for much else, honestly. Between work, taking care of Dad, and now spending time with you. . . It doesn't leave a ton of time for hobbies."

That's unfortunate. And also inspires the best gift idea I've ever had.

I hide my realization behind a coy smile and a continued walk in the market arm-in-arm with my soulmate.

Ash isn't going to know what hit him.

CHAPTER 29

AXE THROWING

It takes the whole week to plan everything to perfection. A week of avoiding deep conversations with Grandma and Hazel during magic lessons. A week of keeping my mouth shut every time I'm around Ash, even though I'm so excited I'm threatening to burst.

A week of Belle begging me to spend the night at Ash's every single night. The spoiled princess.

It's all worth it when I drive up to Ash's house and he's waiting for me in the doorway on Christmas Eve. Wrapped up in some flannel faux-wool-lined jacket thing, hair a little bit longer than usual and perfect for tugging.

"There she is," he says as I step out of the car. "My woman with her mystery plans. Do I get to know the surprise yet?"

He's asked me that every single day for the past week—ever since I told him to keep Christmas Eve night open.

"No. I'm not ruining the surprise after keeping you successfully in the dark for a week. Don't be silly!"

He eyes my car, planting his feet just a little firmer. "I'm not trying to fit in that little Prius, Goldilocks. So, you're going to have to tell me where we're going."

I cock my hip, resting my hand on my side. "Or you can let me drive your truck and actually surprise you like I planned."

He seems to debate the idea as he stalks toward his truck, eyes on me the entire time. "No one has ever driven my truck but me. Not even my dad."

I roll my eyes. Boys and their toys.

"Luckily for you, I'm happy to be your passenger princess. Let's get it!" He tosses the keys to me and by some miracle I catch them before they slap me in the face.

The drive isn't long, but I may have overestimated my ability to drive this thing. It's a behemoth and I swear I can barely see over the steering wheel.

It keeps me quiet, focused, as Ash plays Hozier and Noah Kahan for us.

"Axe throwing?" He finally sees the giant neon sign on the brick building as we pull into the parking lot. "I should probably be offended, but this looks fucking fun."

"This is part one of our evening," I explain, doing the worst parking job of my life. "Because you need more fun. You deserve to drink a couple beers, throw some axes, and spend time just relaxing with your brain turned off."

Ash presses his lips to mine, pulling me closer with a strong hand on my neck. The angle is strange, all cramped in his truck, but the way he's kissing me is so overwhelmingly good that I don't feel the strain in my back.

"No one," he says before diving in for another quick kiss. "No one has ever planned an evening like this for me."

The emotion in his voice is validating and terrifying all at once. I did all this because I care about him, because I want him to feel seen and appreciated.

That doesn't mean I'm ready for the gratitude for doing it right.

"Well, we won't get to enjoy it if we spend all night kissing in the car and miss our reservation. So come on!"

I hop—quite literally—out of the truck and make my way

toward the front door of the bar. Ash catches up quickly, lacing his fingers with mine and squeezing.

I'm so fucking gone for him.

The bar itself is rustic, and almost reminds me of his home in a way. It's not a log cabin, but the walls are wood paneling. The lighting is dark, moody, except for the axe throwing lanes which are well lit. It's very Ash.

"Good evening, may I help you?" A man of small stature asks from his podium next to the front door.

"Yes, reservation under Laura Hollis," I say. "For seven thirty."

He types on his tablet, searching away as Ash's body wraps around mine from behind. It's like the man can't stand to not touch me for longer than a few seconds.

"Gotcha. Your table is this way," the man says, gesturing for us to follow him to a dark red leather booth. "You reserved a private lane for throwing, so it's yours for the next hour. Your waiter will be by shortly to get your drinks and dinner order."

Instead of sliding into the booth across from me, Ash scoots in close on my side. "Want to see who gets a better score out of ten throws?"

My competitive side flares to life despite knowing Ash literally works with axes every fucking day. "Bet."

"Terms?"

"Depends." I lean back to meet his gaze. "What do you want if you win?"

"You. Naked in my bed for forty-eight hours."

My body involuntarily trembles at the thought. "Agreed. And if I win, you have to go shopping with me, let me pick out some things for you, and then take me home and keep me naked in your bed for twenty-four hours instead of forty-eight."

His eyes fill with desire. "Bet."

❧

THE WOOD IS SMOOTH, soft as I lift the axe above my head. I calm and center myself to make the perfect bullseye.

Despite Ash's unending shit-talking, I'm only a few points behind. Enough that I need a bullseye, but that's doable.

I can beat him.

"Don't fuck it up," Ash says right as I'm about to throw.

I stop myself at the last second, glaring at him. "That's a cheap trick."

"All's fair in love and war."

I nod, purely because I know I would do the exact same thing to secure my victory. And that I may have done exactly that when I adjusted my cleavage while he was throwing earlier.

I take a deep breath, closing my eyes. I got this. I let the axe fly and don't open my eyes until I hear the satisfying *thwack* of the axe imbedding itself in the wall.

Bullseye.

"You win, Goldilocks," he purrs in my ear. Electric sparks zoom down my arms as he strokes my skin. "Guess we're going shopping."

"Don't worry, that won't be happening tonight." I turn to face him. "Now, let's eat some dinner and get going to part two of the evening."

"Your wish is my command."

CHAPTER 30

EXTREME CAMPING

We pull up to the next location with bellies full of wings, soft pretzels, and other bar food. I chose not to drink because I'm driving, but Ash had a beer as well.

"What are we doing out here?" Ash asks.

I brought him to the lot leading to the little spot in the woods where we stood and watched the sunrise together. This place was his and his father's, but now it feels a little bit like mine, too.

"This is a safe place for you. A safe place for us. I couldn't imagine crafting the perfect date for you and not coming here to watch the sunrise."

I jump out of the car before I can see his reaction. I hate that I still act like a spooked horse around him, ready to flee at the first sign of danger.

But at least I'm trying, right? I'm making more of an effort than I ever have, and that has to count for something.

Despite my best effort to skip past that moment of vulnerability by grabbing the heavy backpack from the back, Ash catches up to me quickly and envelopes me in a bear hug too warm to resist. "You do realize it's winter, right? I never really saw you as the extreme camping type. Watching the sunrise implies we're spending the night, Goldilocks."

I huff an annoyed breath. "I'm literally a Fire witch, Ash. Do you really expect me to let us freeze?"

He holds his hands up in surrender with a laugh. "Fair point, fair point. Lead the way."

I shoot him one more glare and step into the forest. Even though I've only been here twice, I hold my head high and point-edly put one foot in front of the other, making my way in the direction I think his favorite spot is located.

He quietly redirects me three times before we enter the clearing.

A soft layer of snow covers the ground, but it's not actively falling and the moon hangs full tonight. A cloudless sky opens before us.

I unpack the thick blanket and tarp from the backpack slung over my shoulder and lay them out. We may not get cold, but that doesn't mean a little extra effort isn't needed to keep us dry.

"I see you, Goldilocks," Ash says as he gets a small fire going. "You've got walls around you the size of skyscrapers, but there's a soft heart behind them."

I don't reply.

I don't want to snap at him, to tell him he's wrong or give him my usual safe response of fuck off.

Everyone else gives up on me pretty easily. I say about three to five mean-as-shit things and they back off. Write me off as a bitch and leave me alone.

Not Ash.

Ash has always seen my sarcastic mean-girl act as exactly what it is—bullshit. He poked and prodded at me, but he never pushed me too far. He let *me* come to *him*.

Just like now. He doesn't need me to respond, nor does he expect me to. He just . . . accepts that I don't know what to say and leaves it at that.

I lie back on the blanket, focusing on enhancing the heat of the fire. Ash and I are encased in a bubble of warmth in the middle of the cold winter evening.

"I really do appreciate this. My dad did his best for birthdays and holidays, but as a single parent he didn't always have the most time. It's been a while since I've had someone go to this much effort for me."

I lace our fingers together as we look up at the starry sky.

"What do you want out of life, Laura?" Ash asks softly. "What's your dream?"

I shiver, but it's not from the cold. "No one has ever asked me that before."

"I'm asking you now."

"I like to sew. I like fashion, accessories specifically. I used to dream about escaping to Paris, but now I think I'd just be happy to make them. I don't know how realistic that is, though."

"If I know anything about you, it's that you can do absolutely anything you set your mind to."

"What do you want your life to look like in ten years?" I ask. I blush immediately. Talking about dreams and the future makes me want to know where his mind is at, too.

"Ten years, huh?" He scratches at his beard with his other hand. "I'll be thirty-seven at that point. Jesus."

"You're so fucking old."

"Yeah, yeah," he chuckles. "I want to put an addition on the back of the house. Knock down the wall to the kitchen, add a breakfast nook, and an extra bedroom or two. I want a dog, maybe more if I'm honest, to keep me company in the woods while I work. I'd like to expand the business a bit, although I'm not exactly sure how yet. I want us to be married, maybe have a kid. Maybe not."

My heart leaps into my throat, pounding like a freight train. "Married, hmm?"

I think the scariest part is that I like the sound of it, the picture he's created of our future together. I can see us in the soft mornings in a breakfast nook, with Belle at my feet and some dogs running around. I've always liked animals.

"Gonna make an honest woman out of you at some point. I've told you once, and I'll tell you a million times—you're it for me."

"Ash?"

He turns to me, letting me sink into the deep emerald-green pools of his eyes. "Yeah?"

How do I explain everything that I feel for him? Everything that he does for me?

Hazel never wanted to be my surrogate mother, she never chose me. She was forced into it because she loves me and she knew I deserved better. But that wasn't fair to her.

But Ash? Ash chooses me every single day. He chose me before I even entertained the fact that I would choose him back. He's never made me question where we stand, what he wants from me.

He loves me. Me. The bitchy, prickly person who pushes everyone else away.

I have no words for this. So I kiss him instead. Press love and devotion and *safety* into a kiss that hopefully tells him everything I can't.

I roll on top of him, straddling his hips and pressing more and more desperate kisses to his lips until he sits up, cradling my face in his large hands.

"What can I do for you? What do you need?" he asks, breathless.

The answer is simple. "You."

All I will ever need is Ash Cedar. Even if I can't tell him that yet.

He slows my frenzy, takes over with that quiet, soft dominance that allows me to fully surrender to him. He doesn't take my submission, he coaxes it. Draws it out slowly and naturally until I'm relaxed. At peace.

He presses biting kisses to my neck, leaving little trails of beard burn in his wake. "Every single part of you is my obsession."

His hands tear at my jacket, frustration with my layers overtaking his calm, cool demeanor.

"I can't always be naked," I huff a laugh, helping him remove my clothes.

He chuckles back, thumbing my nipples into sensitive points. "You should be."

Any reply is lost on my tongue as he sucks one stiff peak into his mouth. Any thoughts devolve into a mindless need for more as I grind into his lap.

"These are perfect," he says, palming my breast in his large hand. "Absolutely fucking perfect."

I whine and he moves to the other nipple, sucking hard until I know I'm making a mess of the white lace thong I chose for tonight.

I had a feeling we'd end up fucking in the woods, and I wanted to be prepared.

"Please, more." I scratch my nails along his scalp, soft black hair moving between my fingers.

He nods, moving his attention to getting my jeans off as quickly as he can. He lays me down gently on the blanket as he rips them and my socks and shoes away.

I'm almost completely bare beneath him, while he's still fully clothed, and the dichotomy should not be as hot as it is.

"Just fucking look at you," he growls, hands trailing along my thighs and opening me up to his gaze. "Fucking look at how drenched you are, how beyond beautiful you are. And you're all mine."

I preen under his praise, pushing my chest out and spreading my legs a little bit wider just to hear his groan.

"That's it. Show me exactly how perfect you are."

His fingers trail along the lacy edge of my thong, almost dipping to where I really want them but always shifting at the last second. A gentle tease that has me gasping for breath. Whining and pleading.

He shushes me kindly, finally removing the fabric and throwing it into the pile of clothes behind him.

The patience has left his eyes as he stares at the wetness dripping from me. It's always in this moment that he loses control. When he sees what he wants and can't keep himself from taking it.

He's told me in post-intimate moments that I taste like melted marshmallows and brown sugar and home. That he's addicted to the taste of me.

I squirm, lifting my foot up to push him forward. Anything to get him to move.

It's all the invitation he needs. He dives in, tongue making quick work of lifting me so high I can barely make a sound. He's gotten so good at this—insists on doing it every single time we fuck.

I haven't gotten my mouth on him yet because we're usually both so wound up after that the desire to have him inside me is too important. But not today.

No, not for his Christmas present. Tonight, I have plans for him.

He presses two fingers inside, reaching that special spot as he curves them forward making my entire back bow underneath him.

"Sometimes I think about finger-fucking you with my ring on," he says, lifting his opposite hand and showing me his house crest. "Would you like that? Show me how much you'd like that."

I grab his hair, pushing him back down. Under the direct flicking pressure of his tongue on my clit and his fingers inside me, my head flies back as I cum.

It takes minutes to regain my sanity. To breathe normally after the waves of satisfaction that still send little aftershocks through my body.

He sucks his fingers into his mouth, gathering every last taste of me. "God, I need to be inside you."

I shake my head, hand coming to rest on his chest. "No. No, lie down."

He cocks his head but does what I ask.

Slowly, I remove his clothing. I take everything until he's as bare as I am, moonlight shining on his soft skin. I love him like this. Relaxed, responsibilities left at home. Under the moonlight and trees.

I trail my fingers along his thick, corded thighs, the hair tickling just a little. "You haven't let me take care of you. I'd like to."

He closes his eyes, taking a deep, shaky breath that speaks of desperation. "You're going to kill me, woman."

"That's not a no, but it's not a yes, either. May I?" I lower my head, a hairsbreadth away from the small bead of pre-cum at the very tip of his length.

"Whatever you want. I'm yours."

"Have you thought about it? What I'd look like with my lips stretched around your cock?"

He groans again, hands fisted at his sides. "I've thought about you in every single way imaginable. But I know whatever I've imagined will never be as good as the real thing."

I shrug. "True."

And with that, I swallow him down to the back of my throat. I haven't done this in a while, so I breathe and swallow through the spasms. I pull back, trailing a thick vein on the underside with my tongue.

"Fucking hell. You look so goddamn good."

I put his hands in my hair, encourage him to get a good hold as I suckle at the mushroom head.

"Okay, okay. Fuck. Stop," he breathes, pushing me back after maybe a couple more deep pulls.

I glance up at him, my lips brushing against the tip. "What?"

"While I would love to paint those pretty lips in cum," he says, rising over me like a predator. "What I need tonight is us."

He holds my hands above my head, positioning himself right at my entrance.

"What I need—" he slides home in one smooth, perfect thrust "—is this."

I love you, Ash Cedar. The thought comes unbidden to my mind as it expands, as it encompasses both of us and our passion and love.

Tears spring to my eyes, but I don't want him to stop. I don't want him to ever stop.

I wrap my legs around him and encourage him to show me just how much my love is returned. Even though I'm not ready to say it aloud.

Even though I may never be ready to say it.

CHAPTER 31
CHRISTMAS DAY

Ash and I blink awake at sunrise on Christmas morning wrapped around each other. We did eventually put our clothes back on—considering it's winter and we're in the middle of the woods—despite not wanting to. The fire has reduced to simple embers, but it stayed awake as we slept. Almost as if to keep us safe.

"I could wake up like this for the rest of my life," he whispers into the soft morning glow, breath clouding in the cold. Into the golds, yellows, and pinks that cover the treetops and the pillow of snow beneath us.

"Considering you said you want us to be married within the next ten years, I would hope." The joke falls slightly flat given his sincerity, but he chuckles anyway.

That's just like Ash, though, to make sure I don't feel uncomfortable being myself.

"Within the next *two* years actually, Goldilocks." He kisses the top of my head.

My heart pitter-patters a stuttered beat. "I guess you are old as fuck, aren't you?"

"I've never heard you complain. Hey." He nudges my shoulder with his. "How would you feel about Dad and I coming over for a little after presents this morning? It would really mean a lot for us to spend part of the holiday together, and for you to meet him."

The 'because I don't know if this is his last Christmas' goes unsaid, but not unfelt. And it's that fact that has me nodding. As much as Ash always knows what I need, I like to think I sometimes know what he needs, too. And the way he's looking at me—with hope and a little trepidation—tells me he needs this.

This isn't terrifying in the least. I've never met a romantic partner's family before—most likely because I don't stick around long enough for that to be a consideration—but I'm not envisioning me being a big hit with parents.

"You'll drop me off to my car and we'll meet at the house?" Thank God I'm going to meet his father in a scenario where I can easily hide behind my charming grandmother. Who will probably be unable to say no to extra visitors because I'm springing it on her last minute.

I'm a coward, but at least I'm self-aware enough to admit it.

He hums in agreement, burrowing further into my neck. Soft kisses press against every mark he made last night until I'm breathing heavily and forgetting we're supposed to be anywhere other than right here. "The fucking sounds you make."

Ash is incredibly vocal. Always complimenting, sharing, just talking, and as much as I thought it would be annoying . . . it works.

He rolls on top of me, and I meet the gentle thrust of his clothed hips. "Aren't we supposed to be leaving right now?"

"When you're beneath me, nothing else exists."

"But you bought me Christmas presents and I want to open them." I nibble on his bottom lip but dodge his kiss, giggling to myself.

He chuckles, blowing a raspberry into my neck that makes me squeal. "Presents first. Family second. Then you in my bed tonight. Fair?"

I nod, pulling him into a hug.

I love you.

~

THE HOUSE IS all creaky and happy as I step inside. It's always liked Christmas morning, as I think it was probably the most normal day of the year growing up. Mom actually showed up emotionally.

Well. No. She showed up emotionally as much as was possible for her. Which still wasn't enough, but was a lot more than usual.

I'd even get a few words from her. Which was triple what I'd get on a regular basis.

The inside of the house is covered in garlands. Alive and thriving garlands. They twist around each other and move softly with the twinkling lights of the Christmas tree.

It's like Mother Nature threw up in here. And I like it. Which is a testament to how soft Ash is making me.

Christmas music blares from the living room and I softly step toward the stairs. I'll revel in the festive vibes, but only once I change clothes.

I've been sleeping on the ground, for goodness' sake.

I strip off the cold clothes and snuggle into my red, floor-length dressing gown. It may be a bit dramatic, especially for meeting Ash's dad, but this is me.

I'm not hiding who I am anymore or trying to be anyone else.

But I also wear a tank top and long pants underneath it.

Belle winds around my legs as we walk back downstairs. She probably smells Ash on my skin, the little trollop.

I swear she meant to pick him but got confused by the soulmate bond.

Hazel and Grandma sit in the living room by the tree in pajamas, giggling over coffee. It's a pretty picture, like something out of a magazine.

And I still don't feel like I fit.

"Dear, I barely heard you. Come, sit, we've been waiting until you arrived to open gifts." Grandma waves me over. I delicately sit on the floor opposite Hazel, Belle curling around my back.

"I figured we'd do our gifts now and then when Noah comes over we can do more broad presents," she continues.

"And Ash and his dad," I say.

Grandma's mouth lifts in a conspiratorial smile. "I didn't realize your overnight date was going to turn into a daytime invitation. But seeing as he is your soulmate, I would like to get to know him."

"The more the merrier!" Hazel hands a gift to Grandma.

It's a gentle acceptance that makes my eyes water. I covertly wipe the tears with the sleeve of my robe.

Grandma gives Hazel a smile and opens the box, chortling when she opens the top. It's an animal skull with a long snout. "The skull of an Odocoileus virginianus!" She turns to both of us with a smug smile. "Or more commonly known as a white-tailed deer."

God, they're weird.

"Well, if Grandma is in the spotlight . . ." I say, handing her the slightly heavy box covered in Snoopy Christmas wrapping paper. Most of the inside is fluff to make sure her gifts didn't shatter.

She handles it gingerly, as if she subconsciously knows the contents are fragile. A small gasp escapes her as she sees the tea kettle. "It's beautiful, Laura."

Something warm and gooey unfurls in my chest at the joy on her face. Knowing I did that, that I showed someone I cared about them? After last night with Ash, and today with Grandma, it may be becoming a habit. I don't think I mind.

Hazel scoots the next gift my way. It's from her, if the excited look on her face is anything to go by.

I try to make my smile as genuine as possible as I pick apart the wrapping paper. Inside the box is a bubblegum-pink Brother SE700 sewing machine. It's a beautiful model, and perfect for my hobby of making little accessories.

But it's pink.

Even Ash knows pink isn't really my favorite, and I didn't have to tell him.

But why would she know any different? I've practically shoved pink down people's throats since I was a kid because I know it's expected of the blonde, bubbly baby sister.

I hate that I'm realizing we were never open with each other. We were never real. We may have always loved each other, but we never knew each other.

And we still don't.

It's why everything with Mom was able to blow us apart. Because we were never solid and that . . . sucks.

"It's perfect," I say, instead of everything else in my head. Because it is. I'm the one who isn't. "Thank you."

I don't want to have a sisterly bonding moment, so I hand my gift to her without meeting her gaze. Just like Grandma's I picked out a cute wrapping paper—little presents with smiley faces— and taped it up to the best of my ability. Slapped a little bow on top and everything.

She carefully unwraps the necklace and tilts her head, letting it hang between her fingers to catch the light. "It's beautiful, Laura."

"It's a protection spell."

I don't imagine the little hiccup in Hazel's throat, as if she's trying to hold back a sob. My eyes remain glued to the floor.

"Thank you," she whispers.

Even this feels right. Like I'm taking a step of my own to mend this rift between us.

Grandma clears her throat. "One more gift from me."

Hazel and I both take the proffered boxes. I open mine to find a natural pearl necklace, a vintage piece that certainly has been around for a while. It's just one strand, and the pearls themselves are about the size of my thumbnail.

"Laura, those are my mother's pearls. Pearl is for self-care and nurturing. I'm hoping it will encourage you to love yourself as much as I do." She turns to Hazel as I discreetly wipe a tear from my cheek. "Hazel, that is my grandmother's circlet. She was also an Air witch and apparently tuned it to her magic. I hope it helps you focus your magic as it did for her."

We murmur our thanks, a weird energy hanging over the room like smoke. As if these gifts show we love each other but that love isn't enough to wipe away all the other junk we have to go through.

We have to talk. And that's truly the last fucking thing I want to do. But I've finally accepted that I'm not going to have a real relationship with my sister unless we do.

We just have to actually do it.

A knock on the door captures our attention and snaps the tension in the room like a rubber band, and like magic I know exactly who it is. We've spent enough time together now that I can sense his presence from far away.

Ash. Thank fuck.

I practically leap toward the door, toward the person I love most.

I open the door to his face, and I may have seen him only a couple hours ago but I don't think I've ever missed someone so wholly. My happy smile slips until his eyebrows furrow in worry, and he takes me into his arms without a word.

A throat is cleared behind him. Ash leans back a little but keeps me wrapped in his arms. "Dad, this is my Laura. Laura, this is my father, Birch Cedar."

Birch is practically an older clone of Ash. He's not as tall, but he's just as wide and has the same kind, emerald eyes. His hair is gone, and he's a little thinner than he is in the photo on Ash's dresser, but I know chemo has been hard on him.

"It's a pleasure to meet you, sir," I reply, sticking out my hand and skipping over the jumping jacks my heart is doing in response to being called 'my Laura.'

"I've heard a lot about you, Laura." He grasps my hand. "I hope this isn't too forward, but Ash told me you're his soulmate.

It brings me so much joy that you've found each other. That I'll get to see your love blossom."

So that's where Ash gets it from.

"I always wanted a daughter, you know."

Ash breathes heavily, smiling despite the exasperation. "She doesn't need someone else fawning after her, Dad. She has the entire world eating out of the palm of her hand."

"I am literally right here," I grumble with no bite. I smile as I guide them into the house.

"Birch Cedar, it is so lovely to see you," Grandma says. "Can I get you some tea, some coffee?"

"Some tea would be wonderful, Ms. Pruitt." Birch dips his head to her. He's probably been calling her that since he was a kid.

"This is my sister, Hazel," I say, introducing the only other person in the room.

Pleasantries are exchanged as I burrow into Ash's safety and warmth. Into the beautiful soothing hum of the electric current passing between us.

"You okay?" he whispers into my hair.

I nod. I am now.

He places a big, clunky bag under the tree that I literally didn't realize he was holding and wraps himself around me again.

"Is that all for me?" I ask, blinking up at him from beneath lowered lashes.

His chuckle is deep, rumbling from the center of his chest. "Of course it is. And then your big present is at home."

My heart flutters. "Home, huh?"

He kisses my forehead, drawing me to the couch and snuggling me up to his side. Everything is okay as long as Ash is here.

Soon enough, Noah arrives and the house is full of chattering and laughter—something I haven't heard since my father died. Hazel,

Grandma, and I certainly had our moments, but not enough that the house laughed along with us.

Not enough that the joy soaked into the walls, making the lights brighter and the house warmer.

It's something I didn't realize we were missing until I finally had it.

The house is alive and so are we, despite Mom's absence.

Ash and Noah are in the middle of some lively discussion about something called Warhammer? I couldn't tell you what the fuck it is, but apparently Hazel commissioned Ash to make some minis for Noah when he wouldn't talk to her. And that apparently made Ash look into it and he's all obsessed and asking Noah fifty thousand questions.

Nerds.

It's oddly reassuring that they like each other so much. Like just another piece of our family puzzle has clicked into place now that Mom is gone.

What an awful thing to think, but it's true. It's never been more obvious just how much she was holding us all back from having connections and love.

Her selfishness has never been so painfully laid out.

And yet, I can't help but feel guilty. I can feel it gnawing at me. What kind of daughter thinks this kind of thing? Especially after I read her letter and found that she sacrificed herself specifically to prevent Hazel from turning into the shell of a person Mom became.

I shake my head. I can't do anything to help her right this second.

Instead of continuing to wallow, my fingers trail along the cool side of the sewing machine my sister got me.

Pink.

I huff. I can't really be mad at her for it. I think having Ash's focus entirely on me has spoiled me. Set expectations that my family should know me better than they do, better than I allow them.

"Hazel spent a lot of time trying to find one that color," Noah says, turning from the conversation with Ash.

Hello, crushing guilt, how are you today?

"That was very sweet of her," I reply. It's neutral, but honest. I don't want to lie anymore.

"Pink *is* your favorite, right?" he continues, cocking his head. Noah is perceptive, too perceptive.

Ash leans back with that shit-eating grin on his face that I know spells trouble. "Nope. Her favorite is red."

I pluck at one of the ridiculous fake feathers on my dressing gown.

A shadow falls over my shoulder.

"Hey, baby," Noah says, eyes locked on the space above that shoulder. Hazel.

"Hey," she replies. The guilt in that one word is almost overwhelming. I don't even have to look at her face to know that she's beating herself up for not knowing her own sister's favorite color.

But it isn't her fucking fault. There's some shit she's done wrong, but this? This isn't one of them. And that's on me to make better.

"Dinner is ready!"

Thank fuck for Grandma. Thank the absolute fuck for that woman.

In all honesty, this dinner isn't the most awkward dinner we've had at this table. The bar for normalcy is incredibly low.

Ash and I are side by side, across from Hazel and Noah. Grandma and Birch sit at the opposite heads of the table.

Part of me wishes it was Grandma's soulmate sitting in that seat. She could use some dick to help her relax.

Which is a very weird thought to have about your own grandmother, but it's mostly from a good place. I just want her to be happy, and it feels almost wrong that she's the only one in the family without a soulmate.

She's positively glowing though. A genuine type of non-jealous happiness that I think most families are more familiar with.

"I wanted to thank you for the invitation," Birch says, cutting into his Christmas ham. "It's been a while since Ash and I have had a family Christmas with more than just the two of us."

"Well, you're family now, so you'll just have to get used to it." Grandma nods matter-of-factly. I get the impression that if I hadn't extended the invitation, she would've tracked Birch down to drag him here herself.

A half smile curves along his face, and I'm smacked once again by the resemblance between him and Ash. It's not just looks—it's mannerisms too.

I get the distinct impression that Birch is just as mature and kind as Ash, although I'm not getting as much of the shit-stirrer vibe.

Speaking of.

"You really had to mention that pink isn't my favorite color?" I hiss under my breath into Ash's ear.

He shrugs. "I didn't realize your sister was just around the corner."

"Even if she wasn't, I get to tell them things like that in my own time. It's on me to fix it."

A rare moment of guilt flashes in his eyes as he leans his forehead to my shoulder. "You're right. That wasn't right for me to do. I'm sorry."

I think that may have been the healthiest communication through a mini-conflict I've ever had in my life. The man really is softening me.

"Thank you," I whisper.

He wraps his hand around my thigh, the warmth of his skin seeping through the layers of dressing gown and pajama pants.

It's not inherently sexual, despite the placement. It's more comforting, grounding, securing that we're okay and connected.

Grandma and Birch are talking about something, but my ears don't catch the words. It's like background music.

"Get used to this, Goldilocks," he says, squeezing my leg. "This is what Christmas is going to look like for the rest of your life."

A small bloom of hope unfurls in my chest. It's more than I've let myself wish for. I've been preparing for the bad, always expecting the worst. Keeping Ash away to protect him from a life I always assumed would be full of despair and death.

Maybe I've been wrong. Maybe what I've really been keeping him from is this. A real, whole family. Dysfunctional but loving.

"Can we disappear for a second? Go sit on the couch?" I ask him after we've finished our food.

He nods, explaining to Grandma and his dad as I retreat.

The fireplace is alight and I drag one of the warm blankets down around my legs as I curl up. Ash comes up beside me, wrapping my body around him as we watch the licks of fire dance along the logs. It flickers at me like a friendly wave.

"You okay?" he murmurs into my hair, pressing kisses to wherever he can reach.

"Yeah. More so than I thought I'd be."

"Dad likes you, but I knew he would. He's probably going to spoil the shit out of you, honestly."

I press a kiss to Ash's neck. "I do enjoy being spoiled by the Cedar men."

"I've created a monster. And speaking of." He shifts. "I have to get your presents."

I lift a little so he can stand and rustle around under the tree. He places four bags in my lap, winding his arm around my shoulders. "No particular order."

"You didn't need to get me this many," I insist. Despite loving gifts and shopping, I don't want him to feel obligated. I can shop for myself just fine.

He glares at me until I giggle and pick up the first one.

Tearing through the tissue paper, I finally reach a small box. I pop the lid, and inside—on a bed of silk—lies a pair of ruby-red teardrop earrings.

"Rubies signify courage and passion," he says as I softly touch them. "It just makes sense that red is your favorite color."

I sniffle. "You're getting rather smug about knowing all these little factoids about me."

He lifts my chin with a finger, forcing me to show him how his gift affected me. The tears threatening to spill onto my cheeks. "Not smug. Proud. I am the luckiest man on this fucking earth."

He may be the luckiest man, but I'm the luckiest woman. Period.

I blink away the emotions, glaring at him playfully. "Don't tell anyone I cried."

"My lips are sealed."

CHAPTER 32
IS THIS A SEXY GIFT?

At the end of it all, Ash really did spoil the crap out of me. And that's not even mentioning the gift we are now on the way home to see.

Home.

I almost gasp aloud. When did I start thinking about his house as home? When did I start thinking of Ash himself as home?

Belle *mews* from the back seat. I'm slightly convinced she's a mind reader.

The wooden miniature of her that he crafted sits in my open palm. One of my Christmas gifts, and something Belle spent a little too much time staring at. If this thing connects my mind to hers and allows her to read my thoughts, I'm chucking it in a river.

She *mews* again.

Sus.

"Home sweet home," he says when we pull in front of his house to my arched eyebrow. This totem better not connect all three of our minds.

We dropped his dad off on the way and I can honestly say it was nice being around him.

Birch—or Call Me Dad If You Want—has that quintessential dad energy, despite said energy flagging. The chemo may be a lot, but you can tell the man doesn't let it hold him back. I don't fully understand everything he's going through, and it feels nosey as hell to ask. Look at me being polite for once and trying to respect boundaries.

We love the self-growth.

I let Ash lift me out of the truck, sliding me down his body as he puts me down. I don't think I'll ever be sick of him or how he feels.

I think if it were up to Ash, we'd spend literally every second ravishing each other. Maybe more.

My nose nuzzles against his as I press a soft kiss to his lips. It's all very domestic and sweet.

"You'll need to close your eyes," he says as we enter his home. Belle very quickly finds the plushy bed Ash bought for her and commences her favorite activity.

Ignoring us.

"Do I really?"

He nods, pressing his front to my back and covering my eyes. He walks us around and I'm ashamed to say I've memorized the layout and know exactly where we are.

The bedroom.

"Is this a sexy gift? Is that why you couldn't give it to me while we were in front of family?" I squeal as he pinches my side.

"No," he chuckles as I bat away his hand. "Not a sexy gift."

Before I can keep guessing, he drops his hand and there it is.

A sleek mahogany dresser about as high as my waist. Little engraved flames swirl in intricate dances in all the right places, so that it's not overwhelming or kitschy. Just an enhancement and display of skill.

A small cat sits in the bottom corner, an almost uncanny resemblance to Belle.

This must have taken weeks. Maybe months. Months when

we weren't together. Months he was certain I would be his despite me pushing him away.

"I want you to have a place to put your things. I don't want you to have to lug a suitcase back and forth every time you stay here. I want you to feel like this is another home for you," he explains, scratching at his beard.

He's . . . nervous. Worried that I won't like it, or won't appreciate it. Or maybe that I'll think it's too much and run.

Guilt piles heavy on me. It will take a lifetime to rid him of that fear. Fear that I put there.

I slide my hand along the top. Not a single rough spot. It's so smooth it almost feels like fabric.

"It's beautiful," I whisper. This man really is healing all the jagged, broken places inside me. Even just a few weeks ago a gesture like this would have caused panic to rise in my throat like bile.

But now? Now I see that his love isn't something to fear, even if I do fear losing him.

As long as I keep him as separated from this Mom-is-in-Hell-and-needs-rescuing nonsense as possible, I can keep him safe. But more importantly, I can keep him.

He presses a kiss to my lips, one of warmth and love.

Of home.

CHAPTER 33

PLANNING SESSION

"I'm not going in there."

The Cat's Cradle looms before me, a giant, glaring reminder of all the memories of Dad I don't have. Memories I didn't get a chance to make because he's gone. It's one of the last places Mom was alive.

"We need to plan," Grandma replies, putting her hand on my shoulder. "And in *there* is the best place to do it."

I stare at the brick façade, the slightly bronze-y green sign above the wide street-facing window. I don't want to go in there.

Hazel takes my hand, giving me a soft squeeze. "Why don't you want to go in?"

The temptation to snap that it's none of her fucking business is strong, but I learned something during Christmas. She's not perfect, but I'm not either. I can't keep getting hurt that she doesn't know me, and then turn around and keep her at arm's length.

If I want the opportunity to make this relationship better—and I do—I have to take a step forward. I have to show her who I am and what I feel.

What she does with that is up to her.

"The last time I was here . . ." I take a deep breath, trying to settle the shaking in my voice. "Was the last time Mom was here."

Grandma rests her head on my shoulder just as Hazel squeezes my hand again.

"Together," Grandma says, voice soft and wavering. "Together we are strongest. Together we can face anything. Even this."

I nod. "I'm scared."

A small tear escapes my eyes, trailing down my cheek. Being vulnerable like this with my family isn't something I'm used to, but maybe it can be okay. Even if it's just as terrifying as walking through the front door.

"You won't be alone." Hazel brushes my hair back with her free hand, curling it behind my ear just like she used to when I'd had a nightmare when I was a kid. I lean into the touch. "Let's go figure this shit out."

With one last deep breath, I allow them to pull me inside The Cat's Cradle.

It's the same as the last time I was here. Rows of bookshelves covered in all manner of books, crystals, herbs, and other witchy nonsense. A glass counter on one side with the more valuable items inside.

And memories. They're not a flood escaping from a blocked door this time, more of a kind nudge.

Dad watching Hazel and I run around as kids. Mom showing us different books. Grandma sneaking crystals into the pockets of our jeans.

I grew up here, and I never remembered it.

"I still don't know too much about Hell, girls," Grandma says, snapping me back to the present. "I don't know of anyone except daemons going to Hell on purpose, so this is a tad unprecedented. That being said, I do have a meeting with the Fire witch, Georgette, set up for after New Year's, and I believe she can help fill in some of the gaps in my knowledge."

"No one owns a time-share there? Surprising." Nervous

energy makes me snarky, but the small smile Hazel shoots me shows that maybe she gets that I'm not being mean.

"Can you tell me what it felt like when you were there, Laura? When you were speaking with your mother?" Grandma's voice hitches at the end, but she hides it by flicking through book spines. I don't know if she's looking for something, or just needs something to do with her hands.

"Hot. It felt hot." I wrap my arms around myself despite my words. "It didn't feel like I was actually there, if that makes sense. It almost felt like I was part of the fire, like I was watching what was happening behind a plume of smoke. Mom wasn't corporeal, really. I could just . . . feel her?"

"That's fucking terrifying," Hazel huffs.

"And maybe a good thing," Grandma says, pulling a book off the shelf. "It may be easier for you if you're not really there. I don't love the idea of sending you into Hell after all."

She waves us to the counter where she opens the book. *The Women of the Pruitt Line.* She flips through the pages, obviously searching for something specific.

"Aha!" she says, flipping the book around to show me and Hazel. "There!"

". . . THE PRUITT WOMEN ARE MOST CONNECTED TO THEIR ANCESTORS—AND THEIR MAGIC—ON THE DAY OF ELIZABETH PRUITT'S DEATH. THAT IS THE DAY ELIZABETH WOVE HER MAGIC AND CAST THE SPELL THAT HAS STRENGTHENED THE LINE FOR THE PAST FOUR HUNDRED YEARS."

"OKAY?" Hazel meets Grandma's exasperated gaze.

"We have to rescue Mom on this day?" I guess. "On the day when we're most connected to our magic?"

Grandma's eyes light up, her grin large. "Exactly, my dear. That is the day we should have most success with any endeavor—

but especially one as dangerous as this. And thankfully for us, it's in January."

A little bit of pride grows in my chest. I feel the most confident I ever have in my magic, and it's starting to show in the way Grandma is looking at me. I don't feel like I'm on an island by myself anymore. I'm holding my own, standing on my own two feet, with the witches of my family. Finally part of the planning.

"And what will we be doing while Laura's rescuing Mom? Just . . . waiting?" Hazel paces, frustration bleeding off her. "There has to be a way we're involved, or we can help."

"Do you remember how your mother touched each of us before she banished herself and Draven?" Grandma closes the book. "She did so to connect our magic and use it for herself. If we remain in physical contact with Laura for the entirety of the ritual, she can utilize our magic and be stronger."

Hazel nods but doesn't stop pacing. It's not a good enough answer for her, but considering we're flying mostly blind—it's what we have.

"Maybe this Fire witch lady—" I start.

"Georgette." Grandma's voice is stern.

"*Georgette* will have some more ideas about how you can help."

Hazel stops, turning to both of us. "Are we even sure this is a good idea? This seems . . . risky, to put it lightly. I'm not saying Mom deserves to rot in Hell, but, I mean, she kind of does. Are we sure putting you, Laura, in this situation is a good idea?"

The room goes deadly silent.

The seconds stretch on as we all stare at each other, willing someone to say something. Willing someone to say that me risking my safety is worth it because Mom deserves it.

I pull Mom's letter out of my jeans. Belle nudged me until I grabbed it and put it in my pocket this morning, almost as if she knew I would need it. Knew I'd need to explain *why* I can't just let Mom rot.

I need to figure out just how sentient Belle is.

"Here." I hand it to Hazel. "Read it. Now, or later, whatever you feel comfortable with. But, despite the mother she was to us . . . she deserves a chance."

Hazel holds the letter to her chest before nodding and putting it in her bag.

"So, we're doing this?" I ask.

Grandma nods, and Hazel follows.

Looks like we're rescuing Mom in January.

CHAPTER 34

WILD

New Year's comes and goes. It's never been my favorite holiday, but everything seems better with Ash around.

His dad even made his famous mac and cheese. Which in and of itself seems like a simple dish, but that man makes magic. I have no idea how or why, but I will never eat any other mac and cheese in my life.

I'm still thinking about the cheesy deliciousness as the older, wrinkly woman in front of us feeds another live cricket to her creepy lizard. Georgette is certainly a unique character.

Grandma assured us as we walked in that Dotty was friends with this woman and she was totally above board. But the way she's baby talking this lizard has me side-eyeing the fuck out of her.

We must truly be desperate for information.

Or desperate in general.

"The lizard keeps staring at me," Hazel whispers from my side. We're sat together on the woman's plastic-wrapped couch.

"That's because it's weird as fuck," I whisper back.

She giggles and it's normal and healthy and I don't even mind the death glare Grandma shoots our way.

235

Even that is normal and healthy in a way that makes a little bloom of hope in my chest flare to life.

"You." The woman's curved, old-lady finger points at me as she approaches. "You're the Fire witch."

It's not a question, but I nod all the same.

The plastic crackles as she sits down on an armchair across from us. "And you're hearing voices from the flames."

Jumping right into it, then. "Yes."

"The voice of your mother?" She leans forward.

I nod. Yeah, lady, you have the overview.

"It's not something I have extensive experience with, myself. It's a very rare thing when the fire speaks to me. It means you have a lot of power within you that you hear them so often. And so clearly."

Thanks for the compliment, but it's not super encouraging somehow. Maybe it's the haunted look in her so-icy-blue-they're-almost-gray eyes. Maybe it's the fear in the thin line of her mouth.

"What you hear are the souls in Hell, begging for your help to be released. It's not surprising that you connected with your mother, as your souls already know each other. I expect the intention is to attempt to rescue her?"

Grandma's hand is on her throat, rigid shoulders stock-still. "Yes, if possible."

Georgette tries to smile at me. "I understand the urge behind wanting to save your mother. I'm not going to pretend I can talk you out of trying. But be careful. While you may go in to save one, many will try to use you as a bridge to get out. You don't want to let them drag you down."

"What—" Hazel visibly gulps at my side. "What happens if they drag her down? Drag *us* down?"

The woman's face darkens. "You will lose your sister. She will become a vegetable, as good as dead. A mere shell as her soul is trapped in Hell forever."

"Lovely," I wheeze.

It's not that I thought saving Mom was going to be easy by

any means. But risking my own soul to save hers? Feels a bit fucking risky.

But she did it when the roles were reversed. She risked herself for us.

"I appreciate your time, Georgette. Is there anything else you can tell us?" Grandma's keeping it together, but I can see she's barely holding on to sanity right now. She has to make a choice between risking me or losing her daughter forever. And not just losing her, losing her to Hell. A fate much worse than anyone deserves.

Georgette leans back in her chair, crinkle crackling all the way. "Be careful. Be smart. And don't follow the glowing lights, no matter how warm they may be."

'DON'T FOLLOW THE GLOWING LIGHTS' plays over and over again in my head as we drive home in silence.

No matter how warm.

I don't think I even want to know what the lights are. Or what that means. No, I can pretty much guarantee I want nothing to do with any of that nonsense.

Don't follow the glowing lights.

Even as Belle greets me at the door and the house moans and groans as we enter, that phrase repeats itself.

What kind of lights are in Hell? Other than fire, of course, but I get the distinct feeling that's not what she was talking about.

Hazel keeps trying to pretend she's not staring at me, but I'm so wrapped up in my own head that I don't have the energy to call her out on it.

The three of us congregate in the living room almost by habit, coming together I'm sure to discuss what the fuck we just learned.

Which is that I'm most likely risking my life to save a woman who barely gave a shit about us. Who sacrificed her life for Noah. Who is also our mother.

Wild.

"Maybe there's another way," Hazel finally says, breaking the silence in the way only she can. "Maybe we don't have to put Laura at risk to save Mom."

The desperate, pleading eyes she throws to Grandma even have me feeling guilty, and I'm not the intended party.

Grandma shakes her head. "Saving people from Hell is not something done. Ever. It's not written about, it's not referenced, it's simply not done. If there were another way, we would know."

"But we didn't even know Laura was hearing souls! Maybe there's more to this witchy shit than the books know."

"Or maybe . . ." I clear the panic out of my throat. "Maybe nobody as strong as me, or as strong as Mom, has come around before. Maybe this situation hasn't happened before and we're the guinea pigs. Maybe we have to figure this out for ourselves."

Hazel's face falls, hope seeping out of her faster than I'd like.

I sit taller, putting on my armor of false confidence I'm so familiar with. "Maybe we have to decide if risking me is worth the possibility of bringing her back."

"But that's not fair!" Hazel screams. The door to the backyard slams open in a furious gust of wind that rattles the hinges. Grandma puts her hand on Hazel's, trying to calm her.

I shake my head because no, no it's not fair. But it is what it is.

We sit in silence after Hazel's outburst. I've already decided I'm saving her. That note solidified it. The fact that I'm risking my life doesn't change anything.

"You won't do it. If this is a democracy, then I vote no," Hazel whispers. "If we risk you and it doesn't work, then all we've done is lose both of you. And she isn't worth it."

"This isn't a democracy. We may be a family, but I'm the one taking the risk, so I'm the one who gets to decide." I make eye contact with my sister. The person who really tried to protect me for all these years. "And I know I won't be able to live with myself if I don't try."

"But—" Hazel grabs my arm.

"Did you read the letter?"

Her mouth shuts. I can tell by the guilt in her eyes that she has, that it hasn't changed her mind enough. That she still doesn't want me to do this.

At the end of the day, if it were just me and her . . . I'm not sure what I would decide. But she didn't get banished to Hell because she's a bitch. She got banished because she saved someone's life. She got banished for Hazel.

And that will eat away at me.

So buckle up, Mom. I'm coming.

CHAPTER 35
FOLLOW THE SCENT OF NARCISSISM

Training is awkward.

Hazel hasn't brought up the possibility of not saving Mom again, nor has she addressed the letter.

When someone sacrifices themselves to save your soulmate with the intent of saving you from becoming a bitchy narcissist, you really can't say shit.

Grandma doesn't seem to know how to feel and that keeps her uncharacteristically quiet, focusing purely on the magic and nothing else.

And here I am. Staring at fire and trying to contact Mom.

I'm not trying to save her tonight, but maybe if I can get a better sense of where exactly in Hell she is . . . How big even is Hell? Are there actually seven levels?

"Focus, dear," Grandma says.

It's hard to focus when your mind is running a mile a minute.

The bonfire flames crackle and pop softly, soothingly. Just for me.

Slowly, the noises of the world outdoors soften, and the whispers of the fire surround me. Mournful, angry, regretful . . . The whispers are easier to understand than ever.

But I ignore them. They're not what I'm looking for.

No, I'm looking for the woman who spent my entire child-hood ignoring me. Who mourned and never moved on from the loss of her soulmate. The woman who chose her own perverse sense of revenge over her family.

Just follow the sickeningly putrid smell of self-assurance and narcissism.

Help.

There it is.

"Mom, where in the hell are you?" I ask aloud. I'm still not sure how this bond works, but it feels weird replying using just my mind.

No, not you.

"Love you, too. Now where the fuck are you?"

You cannot do this. Stay home and safe, Laura.

Annoyance skitters over my skin. The confidence in my abilities is overwhelming. Truly. It almost makes me want to take Hazel's advice and say 'Fuck you.'

Almost.

"I'm saving you whether you like it or not, so just tell me where you are," I growl. I've never spoken to Mom like this, but it's easier somehow when she's not standing right in front of me.

I'm with Draven. I can't tell you more than that. I don't know more than that.

Well shit.

Things just got a lot more complicated. But this was always complicated, so what's a little more to spice things up?

I sigh. "Are you safe?"

As safe as I can be. He has no interest in hurting me. Yet.

Well, that's some good news at least. A win is a win.

"Anything else I should know before I risk my life to drag you out of your fun little Hell prison?"

Don't do it. And if you must do it—don't follow the lights.

The connection breaks and I come back to reality. The scent of the trees, the cool winter breeze. The holes my sister and Grandma are staring into the back of my head. Fuck.

"She's with Draven. She's not sure exactly where that is. He isn't hurting her at the moment, but who knows when that could change," I say, pointedly leaving out her parting message. They're both worried enough. They don't need to know that she reiterated the whole 'don't follow the lights' creepiness.

Grandma's hand covers her mouth, muting the sobs she can't quite keep inside.

"As if this wasn't difficult enough," Hazel says, shaking her head in disbelief. "If we haven't already pissed him off, this is going to. We have to plan for retaliation. It's going to be much worse than anything we've already got coming to us."

Ripping Mom out of his fingers is going to ruffle his feathers, that's for damn sure.

"Being alive is enough of an insult to him. He won't be content with just her. May as well really piss him off and hope it makes him sloppy," I reply.

Not that I truly understand what the relationship is between Mom and Draven. The only thing I know for sure is the cute little recap she gave us was sorely lacking in details.

"We have a few weeks before Elizabeth's anniversary that we read about. A few weeks to train, and then . . ." I take a deep breath. "Then we get this over with."

Everyone nods, the deadline falling heavily on us.

"If you change your mind . . ." Grandma speaks softly, but her eyes are hard. As if forcing the words out are the most painful, regretful thing she's ever done. "That's okay."

"I won't," I reply.

"What does Ash have to say about it?" Hazel asks, concern furrowing her brow.

Right. Ash.

"He's my . . . whatever he is. But he isn't me, and he doesn't get to make decisions for me. I'm going to attempt this and he's just going to have to deal with it."

I don't plan on telling him, but she doesn't have to know that. I plan on being so far into Hell that by the time he realizes what's happening, he can't do anything. I plan on him being miles and miles away so that even if he slams his foot on the gas and blows through every red light, he'll still miss it. I don't know what will happen when I drag Mom out of Hell. But if there's any hellfire, you can be damn sure Ash won't be around to get burned.

CHAPTER 36

FINALLY

For some ridiculous reason—between the training and the plotting and the planning—Grandma insists we continue with therapy.

I'll admit that we're making progress as a family, and maybe that's because of things like therapy. But we're doing some important shit right now.

Literally tomorrow, actually.

But it's Grandma. So here we sit once again in Dr. Farrow's house-slash-office.

"How were your holidays?" she asks. The tension makes the air in the room so thick I can't believe it's not butter.

Hazel—who has been sipping the let's-share-our-feelings tea for five minutes—clears her throat. "The holiday itself was actually really nice. The best Christmas I think we've had as a family since Dad died."

Not an incorrect statement.

"That's a strong sentiment." Dr. Farrow crosses her legs. "What makes you say that, Hazel?"

"Mom had such a heavy energy. She didn't really leave room for any emotions other than hers. And hers were anger, resentment, unwavering sorrow . . . None of the emotions you'd want to associate with a happy holiday," she says.

I'm still impressed with the balls Hazel has grown. She may have gone to bat for me with Mom every day, but she never went to bat for herself. And now? Now she is.

Dr. Farrow shakes her head, pen scribbling in her notebook thanks to that magical plant of hers. I'd pay good money to see what's in there. "No, those aren't emotions I'd hope for, myself. I'm glad you all had a lovely holiday."

The silence is deafening. The elephant in the room is inflating until it sucks up all the air.

"How are things progressing with the plans to rescue your mother?" Dr. Farrow finally asks.

"Just fine, thank you," I reply. I don't know why I'm hoping that'll close that conversation, but I can tell by the large huff of breath from Hazel that it did the opposite.

Cool.

"Laura is going to risk her life and I'm not okay with it," Hazel says. She had been doing a good job for the last few weeks of keeping her mouth shut about all this, but that tea.

That goddamn tea.

"I had a feeling the task would be dangerous, but is it truly life threatening?" Dr. Farrow turns to me. I'm glad she actually trusts me to tell her the truth. That softens my walls a little.

I nod. "I'm risking my soul."

"She's risking becoming a giant husk as she's tortured in Hell forever by souls wanting to use her as a bridge."

Thank you, Hazel, for that clarification.

Dr. Farrow's eyes widen. It's definitely not what she was expecting, but to be fair, it's not what any of us were initially expecting.

I just thought we had all gotten used to the idea by now. But apparently Hazel has been holding on to her doubt in a vise grip.

More silence.

"You've decided to proceed anyway, Laura?" Dr. Farrow asks.

Her tone—surprisingly—isn't judgmental or laced with I-know-better-than-you energy like Hazel's. It's just a clarifying question.

I look down at my fingers. "Yes. I have to try. I won't be able to live with myself if I don't. If it doesn't work, I'll pull back. But I'm going to try."

Dr. Farrow leans in. "Why wouldn't you be able to live with yourself?"

"Because!" I huff. "She literally trapped herself in Hell for us! While she wasn't the mother we needed for most of our lives, she was the mother we needed at that moment. And she certainly seemed to show some form of self-awareness in her letter."

"She didn't do it for any of us," Hazel says, practically slamming her empty teacup on the table. "I read the same letter you did, but I don't trust a word of it. She did this because she's obsessed with punishing Draven. She did it so she could take him down."

I turn to her. "Maybe. But she still saved Noah in the process. I'm honestly surprised you aren't a little more grateful."

An angry gust of wind flares around us despite the window being closed.

"Girls." Grandma's weary voice comes from the other end of the couch. I almost forgot she was here.

"No, no." Dr. Farrow puts her hand up. "I have a feeling a lot of these feelings are actively repressed. It may lead to conflict, but it's good to get it out. As long as we stay respectful, it's better to be open and honest."

None of us know what to say to that. But I know she's not wrong. A fight has been brewing for months. Years, probably. And I know it's coming.

If the anger in Hazel's eyes is any indication, it's coming sooner rather than later.

～

WE'RE in the house about three seconds before Hazel rounds on me.

"She doesn't deserve you risking your soul!" she says, wind whipping around her auburn hair.

"What does she deserve? Since apparently you're the be-all and end-all of what people deserve. What do any of us deserve?" I snap. "Did Dad deserve what he got? Did we deserve the childhood we had? Did Mom?"

Belle *mews* from the top of the stairs but doesn't come down. Smart cat.

"You deserve to live, Laura. I've spent my entire life trying to give you the opportunity to live."

I laugh. It's a humorless, angry thing. "So it's not about you wanting to keep me safe. It's about you wanting to feel like you haven't wasted your life. Congratulations, sis! You did."

"I never gave a fuck about me, don't you get it? I spent my entire life fighting with Mom for you. Not for me—for *you*. To give you some sense of normalcy. A real life with friends and happiness."

"I didn't want normalcy!" I practically spit fire. "I wanted attention. I wanted someone in this house to actually pay attention to me. Mom never spoke to me. She spent all her energy fighting you and then I got nothing. She may have never shown you love and compassion, you may have spent every day fighting with her. But there were times she wouldn't even look at me for an entire week. You got something from her, Hazel, and I got nothing."

Tears spring to her eyes but I plow on. The urge to hurt her, to swipe at her, is gone. But I need her to understand. I have to show Hazel the parts of me even I haven't yet faced. I have to show her who I am.

"Stop pretending you and Mom didn't fuck me up just as much as Mom and I fucked you up. All I ever wanted was to be loved and seen, and instead I got the Pink Puke Mobile. Whoop-de-fucking-doo for me. Do you know what happened when you left, Hazel? She stopped. She stopped making dinner. She stopped doing laundry, she stopped going to the store. She just stopped. Not before stealing my keys, forcing me to drop out of college, and turning me into her own personal pet hermit, of course. But she stopped. Lucky me, now I know how to make dinner and wash a shirt, but it's no thanks to you. It's no thanks to either of you."

The silence pours into the house like fog on a hazy night. The truth of how we both felt—how we still feel—seeping into our skin.

"No wonder you hated me so much when I left," Hazel whispers. "I had no idea. I had no idea I ruined your life."

"And I ruined yours. You forced yourself into a box so you could give me what you always wanted. And it took you leaving for me to realize how much you were doing to keep our lives moving forward."

Tears flow freely down her cheeks now, hiccups lifting her chest. "We were just children."

"We were just children."

Hazel takes my hands. "She doesn't deserve us."

"No," I say. "No, she doesn't. But once the anger passes, we're going to regret not trying."

Finally Hazel and I see each other as who we are, and what we feel. We're no longer trying to fit the person in front of us into the mold we expect them to be in. We're on the same page.

Finally.

CHAPTER 37

LIAR

My heart is raw.

Hazel and I spent two hours crying together on the couch. Reassuring each other that no matter what, we love each other, and our bond is stronger than the bullshit we were put through.

But it's hard.

It's so hard to face this and know that I'm risking my life tomorrow. It's hard not to run to Ash and let him soothe all of the pain inside.

So I don't fight it.

I stumble into the Pink Puke Mobile with all the grace of a baby deer walking for the first time and drive to him. Some part of me knows he knows I'm coming.

It's why I don't bother texting or calling.

It's why I know he's standing in the doorway even before I pull fully into his driveway.

I get out and run to him.

I jump into his arms, wrapping my arms and legs around him as best I can. He doesn't even step back to brace himself, he just absorbs my energy and matches it with his own.

"I got you, Goldilocks."

Somehow, I've even learned to love that nickname despite how much it pissed me off the first time he used it. It's special. Unique. Just for us.

If anyone else ever used it, I'd kill them.

He walks us into the house, his plants magically closing and locking the door behind us. He sits me on the island in his kitchen, handing me a glass of my favorite wine.

The wine he poured the first night I stayed here.

"Talk to me. What's going on?" he asks once I've drained the glass.

I meet his liquid-forest gaze and know I have to tell him. Tell him what I've been avoiding. That I have to sacrifice my life to save Mom. But I meant it when I promised myself I wouldn't let him near it.

"I'm going to be saving Mom tomorrow."

His sigh is heavy, emotional, as he brackets my body with his hands on the counter.

"Hazel and I had a fight about it. She doesn't want me to do it, and we finally said all the things we've kept bottled up." I try to chuckle. "Seems like you were right about therapy being healthy."

He sees right through me, though. He lifts his hand and caresses my cheek. "I'm sorry you fought. Why doesn't she want you to do it?"

Deep breath, Laura. "Because I'm risking my life."

His face hardens instantly. His body rigid, shoulders squared as he stares into my very soul. "No."

My heart breaks at the look on his face, but I've already decided and he can't change my mind. "Ash, you can't tell me no," I say softly.

"I sure as fuck can. You think I'm okay with you risking your life?"

"I wouldn't expect you to be." I kiss his wrist. "But it's my decision, and it's the only way."

I watch as the emotions play out on his face. As he wrestles with the desire to get all macho-protective man and demand I not go. He knows he can't make that decision for me. He values my independence almost as much as I do.

Bet he's regretting all that therapy now.

"It's the *only* way?" he asks, some of that hardness cracking.

I nod. "I wouldn't do it if there was another option. But part of my conversation with Hazel tonight was about not pushing. Making sure we're being as safe as possible and holding off if I feel like things start to go negatively."

He leans his forehead to mine. "At least there's that."

"I'm not going to die for her. But I refuse to let her suffer in Hell of all places after . . ." Another deep breath. "Mom wrote a letter explaining that she did this to protect Hazel from becoming just like her. Mom didn't want to continue the cycle. And for that, I have to try. For my sister and for the hope that maybe Mom has learned something."

"I'm going with you."

Knew that was coming. "And if I try to stop you?"

"I'll tell you the same fucking thing you told me. It's my decision."

I love this stubborn man so much. "Tomorrow night."

Because by then, it'll be over. I made a promise to myself a long time ago that I wouldn't lose Ash. That if I was going to give in to this soulmate bond, I wouldn't risk his life in the process.

So that's what I'm going to do. I'm going to lie my ass off.

He's going to be pissed. He's going to call me a hypocrite. And he wouldn't be wrong. I'm a huge fucking hypocrite when it comes to Ash Cedar.

But I can't find it in myself to change my mind.

"I'm going to leave early in the morning to spend the day prepping with Grandma and Hazel. You can come by around dinner time."

"Thank you, Laura."

Don't thank me yet. Not until you find out how much of a liar I am.

I wet my lips, biting just a smidge at the bottom one in the way I know makes Ash's mind blank.

I don't want to talk anymore.

Lying to him feels like black sludge in my gut. I hate it. And I'm done with it tonight.

His thumb brushes my lip, pulling it out from my teeth. "How about we do something else with this mouth of yours?"

Bingo.

I nibble the tip of his thumb, wrapping my lips around the digit for a quick suck. "Whatever could you have in mind?"

"When it comes to you?" His eyes are dark as he leans closer, until our lips are a breath apart. "Everything."

His mouth is hard against mine as his last shred of control snaps, and he kisses me with all the love in the world. Ash is intense in everything. The way he works, the way he talks, the way he loves, the way he fucks.

It's almost too much, having all that intense energy focused entirely on me, but the attention-starved part of my brain revels in it. Revels in the way he never makes me doubt I'm the center of his entire world.

He breaks the kiss, sliding his nose against mine before falling to his knees to take my boots and socks off. He's slow—reverent —as he exposes my skin to the warmth of his gaze.

Hands slide up my leggings, calluses catching on the fabric every so often in their lazy pursuit. No matter how many times we've done this, he acts as if he's discovering me for the first time. As if he's always in awe of me.

"Can't believe I haven't fucked you on this countertop yet." He skips pulling my leggings down in favor of yanking my thick sweater up over my head. "Been dreaming about it for weeks."

This may be the only surface left untouched.

I slide my fingers to the buttons on his flannel, undoing them quickly. "Sounds like we should remedy that."

His chest, broad and strong with a smattering of dark hair, comes into view and I almost bury myself in it. I've always liked bigger guys, but this barrel chest is the best one I've ever seen. Defined, but still rugged in a way that makes me want him to chase me through a forest.

"See something you like?" he chuckles, throwing my bra across the room, where it hits the wall with a satisfying smack.

My fingernails dig into his pecs, leaving little crescent moons. "Yeah."

"Hey." His eyes soften as he lifts my gaze with his finger and thumb holding my chin. "I want you to know something."

"Mm?"

"I love you, Laura Hollis. I'm pretty sure I loved you the first second I saw you, and I'm going to love you until my last breath. I don't expect—or need—you to say anything, especially if you aren't ready. But I want you to know that with absolutely no doubt."

The words stick in my throat like peanut butter. I know I love Ash. Even when he pissed me off, I knew it. But there's something holding me back, something keeping the admission from leaving my lips.

"You're mine," I say instead. "And I'm yours."

"You're goddamn right."

I lean in, reconnecting our mouths and halting the conversation. No more words are necessary.

With a little hop of my hips, my leggings and panties are on the ground and Ash's fingers are sliding through the wetness between my thighs. It's almost obscene the way his fingers slip.

The way this man affects me is unparalleled.

The sounds he pulls from me make it hard to maintain the kiss. It's more of a sloppy press and heavy breathing, but it's so good.

Too good.

"Enough." I yank at his jeans, undoing the button and zip lightning fast. "No more teasing."

"Thought you liked it when I tease you till you beg," he murmurs, nipping at my lip.

I press and pull until he gets the hint and he's finally bare before me. "Not tonight. I need you."

He doesn't need to ask if I'm sure, he knows I am. In one smooth, hard thrust he's buried inside me, and I explode like a firework.

The combination of his feelings and my own desire flood my brain, hurtling me over the edge almost painfully quickly. It's sharp and only further deepens my desperation.

There is no relief.

"I could watch you cum underneath me and do nothing else for the rest of my life."

"Better—" I gasp for air "—better get cracking then."

Competitiveness flares in his eyes as he braces himself on the smooth butcher block countertop. From this angle, I get the perfect view of him towering over me.

I swear he made the counter this height for this exact reason.

He takes both of my hands in his, stretching them above my head and elongating my body beneath him. The other hand anchors the small of my back, pressing me even closer.

My clit rubs against the smattering of dark hair covering his pubic bone, sending an aftershock of electricity sparking through my body.

"That's it." He thrusts hard. "Give me everything."

His pace quickens, his roughness only increasing as he breaks down every single piece of me and puts them back together again.

The kitchen erupts in the sounds of our coupling. In the smack of skin against skin, in the chorus of frantic moans I can't keep inside. In the words of love and sex dripping from Ash's mouth.

It's a cacophony of us.

"This is just round one. I'm going to keep fucking you until the sun rises and you have to leave. I want you to smell me on your skin while you get ready and know that I'm in your corner. That I have you."

A single tear runs down my cheek even as the wave of pleasure rises.

I love you, Ash. Please forgive me.

CHAPTER 38

UNREPENTANT

Ash makes good on his promise. We sleep between rounds three and four for about two hours, and that's the only sleep I get until I slip out of bed at five a.m.

We agreed to do this at sunrise—when Elizabeth cast her spell—so I have to be home by then. I pull on my clothes in the kitchen after pressing a kiss to Ash's forehead.

He's a deep sleeper normally, but this morning? He's practically dead to the world.

Just as I hoped he'd be.

I may be vicious, I may calculated, I may have fucked my soulmate into a sex coma so he wouldn't come after me.

But I'm also unrepentant.

The drive home is quiet. A thick layer of snow fell last night after I arrived at Ash's, but the morning is clear. The sun will shine today.

I only hope I live to see it.

The house welcomes me in with a jolly creak, but I barely hear it over the crackling of fire. I'm drawn to the back doors and there it is.

Hazel and Grandma have created what has to be the biggest—

and most illegal, if I had to guess—bonfire I've ever seen. It's at least ten feet tall, and it's beckoning to me seductively. The flames are almost asking me to come and play.

It calls to me, just like it always does. Literally and figuratively.

My feet carry me forward as I answer the summons.

"No, no!" Grandma waves her hands and approaches, pushing me back inside. "You can't connect yet. Not until sunrise. Stay in here."

"What did you do to it?" I ask, allowing her to herd me like a cattle dog does a sheep.

She closes the doors to the backyard. "Nothing much. I did my own little ritual with some of my personal herb bundles and added them in. Focus, protection, connection, family—that sort of thing."

It's taking all the strength in my body not to run outside and dance around it like some sort of feral cat.

"*Mrrroww.*"

Speaking of feral cats. I turn my gaze downward to Belle, who sits beside me with a glare on her elegant face.

Got it. Go outside, get mauled by cat.

"How much English do you understand?" I ask her, scratching behind her long ears.

I don't imagine the eye roll I get in return. "*Mrrow.*"

"Don't sass me, I'm basically your mother."

She hisses before nudging something at me with her paw. I didn't even realize she was hiding something beneath her.

I crouch down and pick up the compact I took from Mom's room when I first read her letter. It's as if Belle knew I'd need something of Mom's with me today.

"Thanks, Belle." I kiss her forehead.

"So, do we actually have any idea what we're doing?" Hazel asks, emerging from the backyard but quickly shutting the doors behind her.

"We're letting the magic guide us." I snort laugh. "Or something like that."

She can't hide the way her eyes soften at my laughter. At the easiness of it. Something happened last night that has made me shed so much of the anger I feel.

Maybe it's that I know what to expect from Hazel now.

Maybe it's just that I've changed in the last few months.

But watching her watch me is healing in its own way.

Grandma lays her bangly-jangly hand on my shoulder. "You jest, but that is most of the plan thus far. We're entering uncharted territory, my dears, and that means we do not have the comfort of a map."

"But we do have ground rules." Hazel crosses her arms. "No pushing. If you feel any sort of resistance, or see some sort of twinkly light situation, you stop. We reassess. We decide if we want to try again on some other significantly witchy day. Yes?"

Some habits are hard to break, it seems. Hazel will probably always feel a level of protectiveness over me that is more than sisterly love.

"Yes," I say. It's easy to agree right now before we're really in it. I don't know how hard it'll be to pull back once I've connected to Mom. But I will try my hardest.

The first stream of sunlight breaks above the trees in the backyard, a little sliver highlighting the wood floors beneath me.

It's time.

Without a word, we file out to the backyard. To the bonfire piled high and leaking magic in each plume of smoke.

Mom will be resistant initially, I'm sure. But there's no way she won't want to take the opportunity to be free of Hell.

And of Draven.

Although I know we didn't get the whole story when it comes to their relationship. And that's more than a little unsettling.

"Hazel and I will be right here. We'll each have a hand on your shoulders so you can pull from our magic," Grandma explains.

Her smile falters as her blue eyes scan me. She knows how risky this is, but she wants to try.

The conflict is clear in her growing tears.

I don't tell her that I'll be fine. I don't tell her that she has nothing to worry about. I don't tell her that this won't be the last time she sees me with life in my eyes.

We both know they'd be empty promises that I can't make. Shouldn't make.

"Let's get started," I say instead. "Before we lose the sunrise."

She nods and I circle the fire. My instincts tell me that where I stand is important—that every little decision needs to be correct or we'll fail—and I follow them. I trust them.

I trust myself. Trust my magic.

I finally choose the place where the sun will hit last, the darkest part of the yard, and plant my feet.

Hazel takes my right shoulder first, clamping both hands on it in an almost too tight squeeze. Her nerves filter through the touch, but so does her determination. She's not the woman she used to be. She's not the scared-of-life hermit who didn't believe in herself.

I'm proud of her. Of the woman she's become despite losing Dad and enduring Mom.

Grandma takes my left shoulder a beat after, her touch lighter. More hesitant. It's strange having Hazel be the confident one of the two. As much as Hazel has changed, so has Grandma. And not for the better. She still makes her sarcastic quips, but she doesn't own them anymore.

She hides behind them.

I don't know what she'll do if we get Mom back. Worse, I'm not sure what she'll do if we don't.

Their magic flows through their touch, a cooling sensation against the heat of the flame. It's grounding, a contrast that helps me focus. No more emotions, no more worrying. I can't focus on anything but what's in front of me. The fire.

Mom.

I stand close enough to let the heat lick up my skin. To just about risk burning my eyebrows off.

Even so, somewhere inside I know I won't burn. Can't burn.

I'm a dragon. And dragons don't burn.

Closing my eyes, I open my mind. Clear the way for the voices to filter through. I don't grab on to any, though, just let them pass by like snowflakes on the wind as I search for Mom.

Search for the voice of the woman I always wanted more than anything. The one who kept me at arm's length for my entire life. I replay our happiest moments. I remember the scent of her perfume. I try to see her the way Dad did.

Time stops in my small bubble. As I use the fire almost as a looking glass. I'm not in Hell, but I can feel it through the haze. I can't see whatever counts as ground and sky, but I can feel the heat and the souls.

I could be searching for five minutes or five hours, I have no ability to tell. I'm just sifting and flicking through.

Until I'm not.

Until I finally smell her perfume. Feel her sadness. Recognize her soul.

"Hi, Mom." I don't say it verbally, but I know she hears me. "It's time to go now."

"Laura—" she begins, unable to hide the weariness in her tone. She's in my head.

"Mom. If you want me to leave you here—really leave you here—then I will. But I want to help you."

She only takes a moment before replying. "Okay, but I have one condition."

Any empathy I've had for my mother slowly slips out of my body one droplet at a time. One condition? After I've literally risked my soul for her? After I thought maybe she'd taken some ownership of how she treated us?

"What? What do you want?"

"If you grab me, you have to grab him, too."

Him? If she says Draven, I'm turning around and not ever coming back.

"You do realize I'm not a goddamn Uber, right?"

She sighs, as if annoyed I'm even questioning her. "It's both of us or neither of us."

"I'm not—" I start.

"It's Peter. Your dad," she exhales heavily. "And I'm not leaving here without him."

CHAPTER 39

THE GRASP OF HELLFIRE

It's Peter. Your dad.

The words stop me dead. It's the last thing I expected to come out of her mouth.

"He's . . ." I can't finish the question. Could he be alive? Hope rises in my chest, however timidly, at the thought. Can we have him?

"He's dead. He can't come back to us. But his soul has been trapped here, and I can't leave knowing that I'm leaving him behind. He deserves to move on, and that's not happening while he's trapped here. So, if you can't do this, I'm waiting here until someone can," she replies.

I admire her determination. I admire the love she has for Dad. I only wish she loved us half as much.

But she's also right—the horrid witch—I couldn't possibly take her with the knowledge that he stays put. It's both or neither. I don't have anything to connect me to him like Mom's compact, I don't even remember what his voice sounds like. But Dad? Dad is worth the risk.

"Fine. But you first, and then I'll find him."

She makes an irritated grunt. "Fine. I have him right here,

though. He shouldn't be difficult for you to grab. He's just less corporeal than I am since he's only a soul."

No pressure.

I take a centering breath, focus on the magic coming from my sister and my grandmother—they're going to shit a brick when they find out—and breathe out any uncertainty. There's no place for it here.

I envision my body, feel my arms reach out past my little window for my mother. Watch as in my mind's eye I wrap them around her for the first time since I was a little girl. It isn't comforting, isn't the kind of hug I get from Hazel, from Grandma, from Ash. It's just a means to an end.

I pull against invisible restraints. Against the laws of nature— the laws of Hell—to bring her back to us. Mom focuses on me. With every pull she becomes more real, less of an apparition and more like the woman I've always known. Her eyes are visible first, the eyes I inherited. The eyes that stare into me, not breaking the connection.

Slowly, so slowly, she yields. Inch by inch she is freed from the gooey grasp of hellfire. The stink of sulfur fills my nose, but I keep pulling. Keep focusing on her eyes until I can actually feel her touch, feel her arms hugging around my waist, and use the magic I've spent months honing to push her through my fiery window.

And she's there.

I know she is. I haven't broken the connection with Hell, but I know she's there just as much as I know Grandma and Hazel are there.

Mom's hands find the open spaces right next to my neck and squeeze. I shudder at her actual touch. "Your father. You have to get him. Go, please. I tricked Draven into leaving to have some time but he won't be gone long."

It would be so easy to break the connection. To call it a win, to quit while I'm ahead. But I can't.

I can't leave Dad.

I vaguely register yelling. Crying. Emotions from Mom,

Grandma, and Hazel that I can't put my time or energy into or I'll be sucked back.

I have to keep moving forward.

I allow myself to fall just a little further through my window so I can feel the heat, smell the sulfur, and follow what I hope is the trail to my father.

Mom was right, Dad isn't corporeal enough to be an easy find. I feel like I'm digging through dirt trying to find him in the space Mom used to occupy. He couldn't have gotten far in the few moments it took to drag her out.

Could he?

Time means nothing anymore. I have no need for time. I'm merely an entity searching and searching for a voice I wouldn't recognize. With every moment I push a little deeper, hoping I can see. I can do this.

"Dad?" I call into the void. Into space.

And there. A small light. The smallest little light, but it's something that doesn't smell like death, so I focus on it. Beckon it closer.

Hold my hands open for it.

The little ball of light isn't like Mom. She had a body and a voice—everything that made her who she is. This is warmth, energy, and light.

And love. So much love.

Love that overwhelms as it glows and enters my hands. I'm crying. It's Dad. It must be.

I'm so focused on him I don't notice the *other* lights. I don't notice that I'm surrounded. That I've lost my way out.

That in finding him, I've also found countless others. That the lights I was warned of were souls all along, and now they approach like asteroids ready to combust on impact.

Panic consumes me, spurring tears and the knowledge that I've gone too far. I've delved too deep beyond my little fire mirror, and I don't know if I can pull myself out. I'm still aware of myself, but for how long?

Suddenly, I'm grabbed by the waist. I lost the touch of my family long ago, but this? This isn't the souls. It's not the lights. It's something else.

I fall limp, using all my energy to keep grasping on to Dad as I'm pulled. Pulled and yanked until everything is too bright.

Too bright. Too real. Sunlight. Birds chirping. Cold, winter air. Yelling. Screaming.

Crying.

Burning.

Burning flesh. It can't be me. I'm a dragon, I don't burn.

I crack an eye to see Ash. Ash, my Ash, staring down at me. He's wrapped around me, his beautiful green eyes full of worry and pain, his hands grasping at me with desperation, and . . . his beard is aflame.

I open my hands to touch him and see the light of my father float toward the sky. Feel his love and appreciation as he escapes from the scene below.

And I lose consciousness.

CHAPTER 40

BEARDFISHING

It's the yelling that finally drags me from the nothingness of my unconscious mind. There were no dreams, no nightmares.

Just nothing.

Until the yelling.

"You don't care about a single fucking person but yourself!" It's Hazel's voice. Full of anger and bitter tears. "You risked your own daughter's life and now we have no idea if she'll ever wake up! It's been three days, and she hasn't even blinked!"

I'm awake, but I can't force words from my throat yet. Can't crack open an eyelid. Not yet.

"She's going to wake up," Ash's growl rumbles from my left. He must be sitting on . . . the bed? I'm on a bed. I must be.

The blankets rasp against my skin as I register the pillow beneath my head.

He's okay. His arms were charred, stank of burned flesh. Maybe I dreamed it. Maybe it wasn't real. Maybe it was the magic changing my perception.

"I deserve your ire," Mom says, her voice flat and devoid of emotion.

No actual apology—God forbid—just an acknowledgment that the anger is valid. What a fucking trip.

I hear rustling. Maybe walking? "You deserve a lot more than my ire."

Go Hazel.

"Baby, let's take a walk." Noah's soothing tone enters the chat. "Let's take a breath. They'll let us know if Laura wakes up. You coming, Ash?"

I am awake! I want to shout it, but sensations are only just returning to my body. I don't have the strength yet.

"No. I don't want her to be left alone." 'With her mother' is left unsaid, but not unfelt.

The shuffle of steps and slam of a door marks Noah and Hazel's departure.

The following awkward silence proves that Ash didn't leave. I haven't opened my eyes, but I know him well enough to know he's staring daggers into my mother right now.

"I don't blame you for not trusting me. You have every right to hate me," Mom says eventually. The passage of time still hasn't fully caught up with me yet.

More silence.

"Was it worth it?" Ash asks. "Losing the love, trust, and respect of your family? Your daughters probably won't speak to you again. Your mother loves you so much, but even she's disappointed."

A heavy breath from my mother. "I can't answer that for you."

A snort almost escapes me. It puts up a good fight, but my body isn't ready.

"Then I suggest you get the fuck out of my face until Laura wakes up and can tell you what she wants herself."

Even like this, the protectiveness in his voice makes me want to shiver. It does end up raising goosebumps on my skin.

Nothing happens for a few beats, long enough that I'm pretty sure she's going to refuse. But then a chair screeches and the door opens and closes.

Despite how pissed Ash must be at me, he refuses to leave my side. I lied to him and he's still here.

"I love you." The words finally escape me. My first words just as my right eye cracks open to see him framed by the background of my childhood bedroom. "I love you, Ash."

My voice is gravelly with disuse and probable smoke inhalation, but it doesn't matter because Ash's face lights up the moment he hears it.

His beardless face. Even without a beard, Ash Cedar is the most handsome man I've ever seen. All sharp lines and full lips. I barely even notice the marks.

"I love you, too." He scoops up my hand, pressing it to his lips. "Goddamn, Goldilocks, you scared the fucking shit out of me."

"I've been lied to," I whine, unable to fight a smile. "You're going to have to find a spell to grow that beard back because your face is giving me the ick."

His laugh is large, boisterous and beautiful. "Then don't burn my beard off again."

My mind finally catches up to the marks on his cheek. Panic rises again as I attempt to sit up. I need to see his arms.

He sees what I'm trying to do and lifts them for me. It's obvious it's been some time since I lost consciousness because they're not as angry as I'd expect, but they're scarred. I bet that weird witchy healer who helped Hazel is the reason they're not as bad as I thought, but they won't ever look the same.

I didn't imagine it.

Guilt prickles my eyes, makes my vision swim. "What happened?"

He breathes heavily, kissing my palm. "I had to pull you from hellfire, Goldilocks. And I'd do it again."

"How bad was it?"

"I didn't think I'd make it in time. I ran into the backyard and there you were—flames enveloping your skin like a shield. I didn't think, didn't listen, just grabbed you and pulled. I didn't even notice the burns until after you looked at me."

Guilt pierces like a knife. "I'm sorry I lied to you about the rescue. About our plans. I was trying to keep you from getting hurt, and I was wrong."

"You're fucking right you were wrong." His gaze is stern. "And you're never going to lie to me again."

I nod. "Never again."

He must hear the seriousness in my tone, notice the change in who I am, because he just nods back.

"Did I hear—" Mom's head pokes in and her voice cuts off as she sees me awake.

I didn't get a good look at her in Hell, just her eyes. But here she is. A mirror image of me as a brunette and featuring stress wrinkles. No love follows. No affection. No real anger either.

Just . . . apathy.

"Give us a minute?" I ask Ash, squeezing his hand as hard as I can. Which isn't much.

His face hardens. He doesn't like this option, and I don't blame him.

"I need some closure and then you can stick to me like glue."

Ash stands, kissing the top of my head. "I'll be right outside the door. I'll know if you need me."

Yes, he will.

I'm half-convinced he's going to bodycheck Mom as he passes her, but all he does is glare and close the door behind him.

Leaving us alone in my bedroom. How many times has she been in this room in my twenty-one years? Few enough that I struggle to remember even one.

She doesn't speak right away. Just walks to the small wooden chair on my right and sits down, scooting as close to the bed as she can get.

I guess trying to figure out where to begin would be difficult in her situation. That doesn't mean I have any sympathy for her, though.

"I met Belle," she starts. "She's standing guard outside your door. Has been for the last three days since you fell unconscious."

That's long enough to explain how worried everyone is. I know how worried I was when Hazel got hurt.

"I'm surprised she didn't scratch you."

"She tried." Her face falls further. "I'm sorry, Laura."

I had convinced myself that Mom saw the error in her ways, or at the very least could acknowledge them. But what I know now is that Hazel was right. Every word of that letter was crap. Or at least, written at the moment she thought she was going to die and full of things she didn't really mean.

Because when push came to shove, she wanted to sacrifice me to save Dad. She would've been okay with that.

"An apology? I didn't realize you were capable of those. You know, considering they require some sort of self-reflection."

Okay, so maybe it's not pure apathy I feel.

She shakes her head. "I deserve that. I've failed everyone in a lot of ways, but I think sometimes I failed you the most."

"I'd agree with that, but it would be dismissive of Hazel and Grandma."

She tucks a lock of hair behind her ear. "That's also fair. I owe you all a lifetime of apologies, and it's only thanks to you that I have that opportunity."

Anger rises again. That opportunity almost came at the cost of my life, and at the cost of Ash.

"Listen to me. Ash could have died because of you. And I did almost die because of you. Whatever amends you have to make burned up in the flames I pulled you from. You may have given me life twenty-one years ago, but I saved yours. I don't owe you anything—including forgiveness."

I expect pain in her eyes, or some cutting remark, but the woman in front of me just takes it.

"I'll be here if you ever want to try," she replies. "Regardless, though, we do need to plan for Draven. Freeing me—and your father—is going to set him off."

I roll my eyes. "Obviously."

"We're going to need your sister."

"Hazel just went outside to cool off for a second. Not that I blame her."

Mom blows out a frustrated breath and shakes her head. "I didn't mean her, Laura. I meant your *eldest* sister."

CHAPTER 41

BURN-INDUCED HEARING LOSS

"My eldest *what* now?" I better be mishearing things, because there can't be another explanation.

Situational trauma.

Hallucinations.

Burn-induced hearing loss.

"We should get your grandmother and Hazel back inside." With that, she stands up and walks from the room, leaving me with a bombshell the size of a human.

A sister-human.

"Did I hear that right?" Ash asks as he comes in.

I groan. "You're such an eavesdropper."

"You weren't exactly being quiet." He *pssts* to Belle as he sits down, and she hops up on the bed and snuggles into my other side. "Who do you think the surprise sister's baby daddy is?"

I groan again, closing my eyes. "While I'm normally a slut for some good tea, I am not emotionally equipped for this right now."

He chuckles, the sound drawing my gaze to his clean-shaven face. That's going to take some getting used to.

I have no idea how to process this—if I'm even understanding it correctly. I've been through too much and I can practically hear my brain screaming for a break.

Even after the few days of unconsciousness.

The door bursts open in a torrent of wind with Hazel close behind. "*Laura!*"

Her relief—her genuine happiness—slices through me like a knife. I never want to make her worry like this again. I never want to make *any* of them worry like this again.

Ash's hand squeezes mine, compounding the guilt tenfold. I will be better for him.

Noah offers his own concerned grin, but it's Grandma who captures my attention. She drags her feet in a way that would've earned me a cutting remark like 'Ladies don't shuffle' only days before.

She never wore a lot of makeup, but her skin is bare now. Fatigue imbedded in every wrinkle. She hasn't slept since the ritual to save Mom, that much is certain.

While there is relief in her eyes, it doesn't fill her with light like it does Hazel. It's as if she is the husk left over after souls dragged her down to Hell instead of me.

"I'm so glad you're okay," Hazel continues, sitting on the foot of the bed. Her hand rests on my knee, bringing with it the calming sweep of her magic.

I shoot a glare at Mom. "Not as okay as I should be right now."

Both Hazel and Grandma turn to Mom without saying a word, their eyes questioning.

The silence hangs like a weight over the room, heavy and thick. Suffocating like smoke. Smoke I'm all too familiar with.

"Draven is stronger than we ever imagined," Mom says, standing close to the door. As if she knows we're all going to hang her out to dry when she's finished. She needs the escape route. "He's made a second home in Hell for his more unsavory actions, and already had a cage set up for me. It's as if he knew I would sacrifice myself to save my family and planned for that exact scenario."

No one replies. We all simply wait for her to continue in stony silence.

She exhales, shaky, as if she's on the verge of tears. "It's there that I learned he captured your dad's soul and was holding it as some sort of trophy. That's when I started calling for help. If it were just me, I would've stayed there for an eternity to keep him away from you all—but I couldn't do that to Peter."

Nice to know her love for Dad is still more important than the rest of us. She's nothing if not consistent.

"In the time I was there, I realized that the four of us witches—"

"Five." Ash's voice shatters silence and trembles the ground. "Five of us witches."

Mom visibly retreats into herself. "Five. The five of us witches can't defeat him alone. We need all the Pruitt witches we can find. We need . . ."

She trails off. As if admitting whatever this sister thing is to Hazel and Grandma is worse than admitting it to me. I'm the one who led the charge to get her back. I'm the one who actually went to Hell, but she's still treating me like a little kid. It stings.

If I were standing, I would stomp my feet. "Just spit it out!"

"Your sister. We need your sister," she whispers.

A beat of quiet. Two.

"We need *who*?" Hazel asks from her perch on the bed. More confused than angry. If this conversation goes where I think it's going, the anger will come swiftly.

Grandma's as stiff as a statue.

"Before I met your father, I . . . I had a little girl. And I gave her up for adoption."

Hazel's mouth drops so low I swear it's going to hit the ground. "Before Dad. That means she's our half sister."

"And I have one guess as to who the baby daddy is," I say. It's obvious.

"No." Hazel shakes her head. "No, no, no. Nope. No. Nuh-uh."

Denial is a river in Egypt, and Hazel is happily sailing away.

"How?" The quiet word comes from Grandma. The first word

I've heard her say since I woke up. It's small, heartbreaking, and so unlike her.

Mom stands up straighter and lifts her chin in the air. "Draven and I were friends, but sometimes things happened. And when I got pregnant, I knew better than to tell him. I cast a glamour and stayed at my apartment as much as I could. I wasn't coming home that often those days anyway. It wasn't that hard to hide."

It wasn't that hard to hide. What a line.

"So we're on a mission to find our half sister to get her to help us kill her dad. Because that seems absolutely logical and likely to happen. What could possibly go wrong?" I throw my arm over my eyes. "Can I go back to being unconscious now?"

Ash snickers from my side for a second before trying to hide it behind a cough.

"We'll lose without her. We have no other choice," Mom says, full of that arrogance she's basically famous for.

"What exactly happened in Hell? What were you and Draven doing down there for so long?" Hazel asks in a way that makes me peer out from underneath my arm.

She's staring at Mom with accusations I have no words for. With implications that I have no interest in addressing right now.

Mom sniffs, refusing to make eye contact. "Nothing. What matters is that I'm back, and he is going to be furious once he realizes what we've done. We have to focus on protecting ourselves."

As contrite as Mom appeared to be initially, she's certainly back to her usual defensive, non-committal self. She'll never change.

"Once I'm back on my feet, I'm going to be moving in with Ash." I may not have asked him if I could move in, but I can't imagine he'll say no. And honestly, there's no way I'm staying in Mom's house after this.

She and I are done. I'll help protect the family when the time comes, and I'll continue being close with Hazel and Grandma, but that's it.

"What a coincidence," Hazel says, smiling at me. "Noah and I have been talking about renting our own place. I think we'll finally take the plunge."

Looks like times are changing.

Mom finally gets exactly what she wants. To be alone in that house with only the memories of Dad to keep her warm.

CHAPTER 42

SANCTUARY IN THE WOODS

It takes a week for me to feel strong enough to leave the house. A week in which Ash barely leaves my side, and when he does it's only to move my stuff to his house.

Of course, the absolute weirdo insists on doing it all himself and not asking Grandma how she does it magically. Something about 'tender loving care' and 'We don't need to bother her.'

I can't fight him on that second point. As miserable as I am being in the same house as Mom, Grandma hasn't been seen since Mom announced her bonus baby.

I worry about her alone in that fairy-tale cottage of hers. But she's not responding to texts other than to say she just needs time. I'm trying to be emotionally healthy and respect boundaries and all that, so I'm letting it be.

Emotional growth is hard.

"Are you ready, Goldilocks?" Ash asks.

I've been standing in the foyer of the house I grew up in—listening to it groan and creak—for a few minutes. The house has been something of a friend for the last twenty-one years. As much as I know it's time, part of me feels like it's wrong to leave.

Mom isn't around. She said something about needing to go

289

shopping before practically fleeing the house. I think she may be offended or hurt that I'm leaving her after all this.

But I don't expect her to understand the bridges she's burned. I don't expect her to show empathy or see past her own nose long enough to acknowledge my feelings.

And I deserve better than that.

"Yeah." I smile up at him. "I'm ready."

He squeezes my hand, the last of my bags slung over his shoulder. Ready to take me with him to our home.

To our little sanctuary in the woods.

It's hard not to reflect on the past few months as we drive. As the snow-covered trees flick past.

I was so angry. So neglected and raw that all I knew was how to fight. I just wanted to push the people I loved away so I could prove that they'd abandon me. That I was right all along not to trust them.

It's so obvious now, but I couldn't see it then.

I'm a bad-bitch witch, with a sassy sense of humor. But I was using that humor as a weapon, not as a way to connect and laugh with the people I love.

I'm going to keep seeing Dr. Farrow as well. Make a point of actually taking care of myself, because the person I am now is someone I enjoy, and I'd like to see more of her.

"You're quiet," Ash murmurs, hand resting on my thigh. "It's unlike you."

I trace the small burn scars that don't look much different than his veins with a pang of guilt. "You like when I talk too much."

"Yeah. Yeah, I do. What's going on in that gorgeous head of yours?"

"I'm just thinking about how much has changed. Externally and internally. And how much more change is to come."

"Your half sister?" he asks, squeezing me. "And Draven?"

My half sister. I've barely processed that bit of news. I knew my mother was capable of a lot, but having sex with a warlock and hiding an entire pregnancy is a whole different level. It's not this half sister's fault, of course, but yikes.

"The two big unknowns. I'm not good at opening up to the people who genuinely love me, how am I supposed to relate to some stranger? And how are we going to convince her to help us? I can't imagine Draven would kill his own daughter, so would she really be in the same danger as us? Is it even fair to ask her to help us? To put her in that position?"

He sighs. "It's a lot of unanswered questions. And you're not going to know how this is all going to go, until you know."

I glare at him.

"I know." He grins.

I sigh. "How about instead of worrying about some half sister and murderous warlock we just . . . enjoy our home and fuck in the shower?"

"*That.*" He turns to me as he parks in front of our house. "Is the best thing I've ever heard you say."

"Even better than 'I love you?'"

His eyes soften as he leans in, our mouths just a hair apart. "No, Goldilocks. There's nothing better in this world than hearing you say you love me."

CHAPTER 43

ONE MONTH LATER

I didn't expect to be nervous. Confident-as-hell Laura getting nervous over selling a few scarves at her soulmate's booth? Couldn't be me.

And yet here I am, practically trembling like a baby fawn in the woods. All because I'm sticking my neck out and showing the world the dream I've kept secret for so long.

Hazel's new booth is only a couple down, and I actually told her via text that feeling her magic so close is comforting. Look at me admitting I love people and enjoy their reassurance.

Who is she?

My gaze flits across the smaller table I've set up next to Ash's larger one, to where he stands talking to a potential customer only a few steps away.

I don't think I'll ever get used to the sight of him, to the way he makes me feel. Even now, when I spend basically all my time with his overgrown self, he can still catch me off guard with how happy he makes me.

Slush sticks to his boots, February snow persisting despite how ready everyone is for spring. And what a spring it will be. Draven has been quiet for now, but we all know that's going to change sooner rather than later.

293

Hazel and I have agreed that finding our sister is important, but that we can't force her to help us. We still want to know her, whether she fights alongside us or not.

Mom told us before I left the house that she didn't get involved with the adoption further than signing over her legal rights, so we don't have much to go on, but Hazel has been working with Grandma to figure out some sort of magical woo-woo to find her.

Which allows me to focus on my own little dream. The one I gave up on a long time ago.

"You ready, Goldilocks?" Ash sidles up next to me, winding his customary arm around my back. Electric sparks fizz along my skin like a familiar friend.

I nod. "Ready."

EPILOGUE – CHARLOTTE

Anger. Rage. The rising tide of an uncontrollable sea monster of legend.

It lives underneath my skin.

It can't control me.

I won't let it.

About the Author

Zoe Shae has always been fascinated by stories. Whether she was creating them with her father, or reading them, they have always been a constant. Creating them now is a dream come true.

Zoe enjoys writing, singing, reading, info-dumping about her special interests, and spending time with her family.

Please follow her on social media—@authorzoeshae—for updates.